Praise for
The Will to Whatevs

"I laughed out loud reading this. I was reading it in public. Three cute girls at a nearby table laughed at me. I swear one of them mouthed the words, 'fat loser' to her friends. I now hate Eugene Mirman."
—Patton Oswalt

"This book is a knee-slapper, a gut-buster, and a side-splitter. Don't read it unless you have health insurance!"
—Kristen Schaal

"Let's face it. You can only get so far in life by dressing just like Eugene Mirman, imitating his voice, and wearing a very realistic rubber mask modeled on his face. If you really want to be happy, you have to inhabit his very mind. And now, at last, this book allows it! At last, now, you can be truly happy, the Mirman way. Just be sure to adjust your rubber mask eye holes to READ MODE, or else this book will not help you."
—John Hodgman, author of *The Areas of My Expertise*
and *More Information Than You Require*

"This book is good, and not just because it was free. Knowing what I know now about the quality, I would have paid at least nine thousand dollars."

—David Willis, cocreator *Aqua Teen Hunger Force*

"A work of penetrating insight and rigorous scholarship. By turning our attention away from the 'will to power' and toward the more deeply significant 'will to whatevs,' Mirman reshapes the debate in a way that will doubtless influence philosophers for generations to come."

—Joshua Knobe, professor of philosophy and cognitive science at Yale University

"Do you need tips on how to live? I mean besides the breathing and eating part? Then this book is for you! Includes self-help tips for Jewish robots from the future (I'm guessing)!!!!!"

—David Cross

"I have read a number of self-help books. This one will help anyone's self. Reading this book is like having a tiny Eugene riding on your shoulder and whispering his advice in your ear. I agree with Eugene on all aspects of this book except taking acid at an office party. I am never doing that again. Buy this book."

—Zach Galifianakis

THE WILL TO
WHATEVS

EUGENE MIRMAN

THE **WILL** TO

WHATEVS

A Guide to Modern Life

HARPER ● PERENNIAL

NEW YORK • LONDON • TORONTO • SYDNEY • NEW DELHI • AUCKLAND

HARPER ● PERENNIAL

HarperCollins books may be purchased for educational, business, or sales promotional use. For information please write: Special Markets Department, HarperCollins Publishers, 10 East 53rd Street, New York, NY 10022.

FIRST EDITION

Designed by Joy O'Meara

Library of Congress Cataloging-in-Publication Data is available upon request.

ISBN 978-0-06-134618-7

09 10 11 12 13   OV/RRD   10 9 8 7 6 5 4 3 2 1

This book is dedicated to my family . . .

My father, Boris, who taught me that to be a man you need to be strong, wise, and have a clean room (or something like that).

My mother, Marina, who worked very hard so that I could live in America and make fun of dating, high school, dance clubs, and public officials, with barely any fear of government retribution.

And to my brother, Ilya, who tried to suffocate me when I was five months old, but then had a change of heart and became a wonderful sibling and role model.

Thank you all very much for your love and support. I love you.

Now, let's fuck shit up!!!!!!!!!!!!

Contents

CONTENTS

Preface

"Life is like a bus: you get on, you get off."

—Eugene Mirman, from his forthcoming philoso-novel,
Okay Life Similes

Most life advice books tell you to do a few basic things to be happy. They can be summarized as: be open; don't be an asshole; lead a life of purpose, free of psychological self-abuse and don't be afraid of trying stuff.

In this book I will go far beyond that—I won't just give you a vague blueprint, but several specific things you can do to accomplish these—and virtually all—goals—from life's beginning to end (and beyond). I call it a Life-Print. No, I don't. Okay, yes, I do.

Of course you'll be happy if you follow what I say, but more than that, you'll become what I call a Self-God. That's a term I made up. I'll be making up terms all the time, so get used to it, Mr. Normal (not a term, but a mild insult—don't confuse the two, please).

Let me give you a bad example of the kind of self-made power I'll grant you. Before I truly begin this book, I would like to write the word *hat*.

Hat. I did it—twice (once now and once when I originally said I wanted to write it). I set a goal, and I accomplished it. That wasn't so hard.

Soon, if you follow my . . . ????? (I honestly don't know how many) -step program, that's how easy it will be for you to be rich, married, or Chinese. (I teach many things, among them, the ancient art of Race-Changing.) Get ready to take a long, hot shower of wisdom. You may want to wear a bathing suit, (1) in case someone walks in while you're reading, and (2) to protect your privates from my scalding, steamy knowledge.

After you read my book, you will laugh at how unfulfilled self-actualized people are—because you will be Over-Actualized, a form of self-actualization that is 245 percent better than regular Maslovian actualization. You won't be able to move things with your mind (except your penis, breasts, arms, etc.), but you will master . . . the Will to Whatevs.

Preface II

The Treasure of Preface Island!

This book is a guide to living life the *right* way, like the Bible is for crazies and weak people (JK, bro), this book should be to you. If it is funny at times, so be it. But please, consider this mankind's defining guidebook from the early part of whatever century this is—like a balls-out *I Ching* or something.

I won't bullshit you. Countless (not literally) books tell you how to fix whatever has fucked you up bad (generally school and an awkward sexual encounter—sometimes both), start over, move forward, and become what you want. They all tell you to be confident, follow through with your dreams, take calculated risks, and you'll be happier, more accomplished, not as much of a nutcase, and possibly married.

Do that.

Did you?

No?

Do it now.

[*One month later.*]

Great. Congratulations.

Now that you're happy, we can move on to all the little things that turn a man (or woman!) into an Over-Man-Woman. You're not going to be a student or a teacher, but a *stu-cher*—because we're all both. All we're doing is taking off our guard and going for a swim in a river of ideas. (I will clarify what I mean in a later chapter—sadly, it may be a much later chapter in a different book, maybe even someone else's book when they aren't looking.)

Let's start at the beginning of conscious life. Obviously, this book is not for babies—they can't read, and they can't plan ahead. It is, however, for everyone else, starting from kindergarten on.

Wherever you are in life, you can skip ahead to the chapter you need to, though I'm glad you're here with me at the beginning. Still, if you need a job and need it fast, go, open your wings and fly—soar in Life's skies on the wings of my advice. (Whatever I ate a few hours ago that makes me an asshole is finally kicking in.)

If you're thirteen and Jewish, or sixteen and other, or older, you can read and use this book right away. However, little kids and tweens can't. They need your help. So all I ask is for parents (and bartenders—if the children are sneaky drunks) to read this book and explain the helpful points to them. There is so much advice I have for young people that they can't access on their own. Thank you.

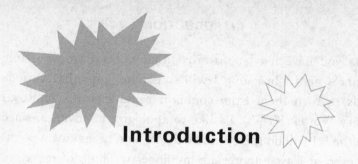

Introduction

When I was a growing up, I had a lot of problems. I was inse-
cure, nerdy, awkward, etc. My troubles went away senior year
after I paid a cheerleader a thousand dollars to date me for one
month, instead of buying a telescope. This is not true. It is the
plot of *Can't Buy Me Love*. That was your first lesson: even if
an author claims to be omniscient (which I don't think I have
yet), he may not be. In life, not all lessons come with clear examples. But all examples have a lesson. If you are in a metal
band and would like to use some of those last sentences in a
ballad, you have my permission.

At the age of sixteen, I read Ayn Rand's *The Fountain-
head* and everything became clear. Thanks, Ayn, your simple
worldview helped me understand the world perfectly for eight
months. Around the same time, I began working at a peer
counseling center and crisis hotline—because sometimes if you
help others, you also help yourself.™ (I have trade marked the
entire book up until now, so don't use the last several pages as
the slogan for your product—it would be illegal.)

Mostly, from my counseling experience, I remember that
people shouldn't have asked me over the phone about sex, pregnancy, or drugs. But I had a nice time chatting with confused
teens and learning about the body. It taught me how to Listen.
And listening is the key to Hearing.

As you have maybe surmised (that's a real word; I stole it from a nerd I beat up), I will sometimes capitalize various words to turn them from common peasant words to Royal Theory Words (RTWs). I'd like to apologize in advance, since sometimes I will do this to create the illusion of making a point. However, at least I appreciate my honesty. Think of me as an impetuous Hegel, drunk with power, and also, regular drunk.

I will, as self-helpers, psychologists, philosophers, and religious leaders (we'll call this whole group Mind Thinkers from now on) before me have, make up words and confidently come to reasonable, but poorly Defendtastic conclusions. I even made up the word Defendtastic. However, I ask you—did I make it up—or did I *Will* it up? Pretty big difference, I'm going to insist.

In the interest of full disclosure, there are three things this book *cannot* help you with: retroactively enjoying junior high school, surgically moving your eyes into your hands in a way that no one notices, and being an extraterrestrial. (You have to be *born* on another planet. Sorry.)

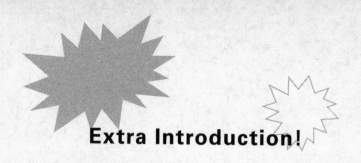

Extra Introduction!

In this book I will teach you, based on stuff I have either made up, observed, or overheard, how to live the life you want—the life you *Will*. Obviously, if your name is Will and you are slow, this book will be confusing/upsetting. Be careful. Thanks.

More Extra Introduction!

What Is This Book?

....

Every era has a book of this kind—at times a book of hard-nosed practical advice or a spiritual behemoth, often asking more questions than answering, but also, often giving various weird guidelines involving food, sex, clothes, and relationships. This sort of book has gone by many names—the Torah, the Bible, *Chicken Soup for the Soul, The 7 Habits of Highly Effective People, The Bourne Identity, Thus Spoke Zarathustra* —not to mention the songs of Mötley Crüe, which answer most of life's fucking and financial questions.

Being a human being necessitates a myriad of Beginnings and Beings. Sorry to Zen you in the head with my Fist of Circular Logic. I was bullshitting you to wake you from your Complacent-Mind-Slumber. Awake, Pupil-Friend!

Let's start anew. Life is goals—Purpose-Attempts—Struggle-Dreams and Accomplishmenties. It sounds confusing (my fault), but it's actually simple. Let's look at two examples:

1. David the WASP wants to be president of the United
   States. He has a discolored penis, which psychologically

tormented him as a child, but now is a source of self-confidence.

2. Jeff the intoxicated sailor wants to go for a swim. He is somewhere in Idaho tied to a chair (at his own request).

Aside from their obvious differences, both are goals, and both require engaging Life-Actions that follow a Goal-Plan to accomplish a Purpose. Admittedly, one is easier to accomplish than the other.

My book is the first modern, straight-shooting, no-bullshit book that really tells you how to do what you want—whatever you want—at any point in life—and even a little in death. Shame on books like *The Secret*, with their confusing double-talk, empty promises, and disregard for solid, honest help. I present here, for you, my friend, reader, apprentice, and maybe lover (depending on your gender, age, and maneuverability), my straight-ahead, no-frills, reality-bending Modern Self-Empowerment Life Guide.

THE WILL TO
WHATEVS

Eugene, Who Are You, and What's This Will?

> **"My book is very funny, but disorganized.
> I think in the end, people will compare me
> quite negatively to a retarded Mark Twain."**
> —Eugene Mirman, drunk in a swimming pool, March 2008

As you know, a good book starts with a good anecdote. The same is probably true for a bad book—that's the fault of formatting. Before the anecdote, you'll often find a preamble about humanity, followed by the answering of several rhetorical questions. Look no further than the book (not film!) version of *Clear and Present Danger*, or the liner notes of any Velvet Underground box set. Though my examples may be untrue, I've certainly prepared you for a preamble, an anecdote, and a rhetorical Q&A, so that's good. Information is best sneaked into people's minds, not told.

Our society is at a critical point in history (if you believe in linear time). Some believe that America and the world are on the verge of global self-destruction—morally, environmentally, sexually, and/or gastrointestinally (*foie gras*—more like, *f-uh-oh gras*).

However, optimists look at mankind and see a civilization on the verge of interstellar space travel, world peace, and the end of poverty. (Those people, of course, are Gene Roddenberry, Bono, many college undergrads, and a handful of charming scientists. Oh, and Bill Clinton!)

> "Mankind is awesome, but weird. Life is confusing: A box full of different things."
> —Eugene Mirman, reflecting quietly to himself while having sex with a group of wealthy tourists in 1995 and then again in 1998

Of course, there are those who don't care either way—they simply want to make out in a bar with an okay-looking friend-of-a-friend. (I am very much in all three camps, which is why *Forbes* magazine voted me the third-most well suited to write a life advice book.)

Throughout our history, humanity has been plagued with questions, and also plagued with regular plagues. I don't know much about biology, so I can't speak to actual plagues. However, I can answer all kinds of questions: moral, ethical, job-related, child rearing, party etiquette, romantic, technological, stuff about boobs, and my three faves: *How do I have sex with someone and not talk to them again?*, *Can you hit a kid for a very, very good reason?*, and of course *How do you get a self-righteous asshole to shut the fuck up, even if they're right?*

Sadly, like many life coaches, psychologists, preachers, and philosophers (Mind Thinker alert!), no matter how much I "get it," it's almost impossible to apply that knowledge to my own life. I'm not so arrogant as to overlook that fact. (On a quick side note, I would argue that—much like Samuel L. Jackson—I am not arrogant at all; I'm just *actually* really, really great.)

It's easy to sit on a mountaintop and tell people what to do and how to be happy. I have chosen to do that. *Not* because it's easy, but for a different reason, which I would reveal, if your mind was ready to handle it, which it isn't, which is also very convenient for me.

Often, what people need in their life is an outside perspective—someone who can tell you how it is. Sadly, since life doesn't take place inside the TV show *Buck Rogers* or the movies *Crazy People* or *The Matrix*, and you don't have the luxury of either a wise-ass astronaut from the 1970s, truth-talking mental patients, or Laurence Fishburne helping you see things differently, you need me.

I am a traditional outsider. I am an immigrant (from Russia!) and a Jew (sorry). I am a comedian—a role historically known for entertaining through its critical, outsider look at society *and* for popularizing fart noises on stage and screen (but disregard the second reason since it does not help with my point). Here I am, like in the days of olde, when jesters were granted special permission to tease kings and right wrongs. (I think that's only part true.) Alone I come with the tools *and* teases you need to survive school, find love, get a job, reach nirvana, or whatevs you like. Kind of sort of? No! Definitely sort of!

Still not convinced I'm an outsider? Or not convinced I can help? Well, let me address your first doubt with a story. (The second doubt can only be assuaged with a leap of faith and a box of wine. . . .)

> *"Sometimes to make a point, you need a story that illustrates it. However, there is always the risk of the story not totally making the point you want. So you should always consider lying—but then not do it."*
>
> —Eugene Mirman, while riding a stolen motorcycle on Route 128, headed to Rockport, Massachusetts, to buy a gun and some painted sea shells

A Story About Someone from High School

··

A few years ago I got an e-mail from someone I knew growing up. He was always very mean to me (because I was a weirdo, a Russian immigrant in the '80s during the cold war, terrible at lacrosse, and not very sexy). In tenth grade science class, he threw fire into my hair. It's important to note that he wasn't an emotionally troubled pyrokinetic (which I would've forgiven even at the time), but simply a crappy kid who lit a bunch of paper with a Bunsen burner and threw it into my hair.

We fell out of touch after high school, because (1) we weren't friends, and (2) he threw fire at me and was mean to me for about a decade. Still, I once ran into him our sophomore year of college, and he seemed perfectly nice and was studying law. Also, a year prior, he sent me an e-mail congratulating me on a commercial I was in. It was a really great commercial, so I understand why someone would want to reach out and congratulate me. That was it, though.

Seventeen years later, he e-mailed me wanting to meet up, get a cup of coffee and talk. I was a little nervous. I knew he wasn't going to hit me or throw fire in my hair, but I was worried he wanted to start an improv troupe. (The spouses of cops and soldiers fear getting a call that their loved one has died; comedians mostly fear a call from someone from their past wanting to start an improv troupe.) He told me he would come anywhere to meet me. I told him I lived in New York. He said he'd come anywhere *in the Boston area* to meet me.

After exchanging a few e-mails over a month, I finally asked him what he wanted to meet about. He responded that he just wanted to say he was sorry for how he behaved throughout our childhood. (He didn't remember throwing fire in my hair, which is awesome, because he wanted to apologize for other terrible stuff.) The next time I had a show in Boston, he came.

He explained his deep regret (this is where the outsider stuff comes in!), saying that his parents were also immigrants (bam!), and that we were both "outsiders," and that instead of being enemies, we should have been friends. He *literally* called me an outsider. How much more proof do you want than a mean guy from my past, in his thirties, seeking me out, to tell me he is sorry for the monster he was and also that I, Eugene Mirman, am an outsider?

What brought this on? Basically, he had quit drinking, and was in stage nine of AA, where you look back on your life and try to apologize to those you've wronged. Now, I doubt he was a drunk in j-high and high school, but once he sobered up and thought about his entire life and all those he knew, he wanted to say he was sorry to a fellow outsider—me.

At the end of our ten-minute conversation (he bought me a Scotch—yes!), I told him that I wasn't upset at all—that I remember running into him in college and he was very nice. I was at peace with it; I'd taken his hatred and insecurity-driven malice and turned it into fame, money, and of course, pussy. I think he felt much better.

Not outsider enough? Well, how about the time I ran for senior class president in high school (and thankfully lost, but just by a tiny bit) with the slogan, "It's not just a change, it's a mutation." Wow. Pretty outsider shit, huh?

> *"This would be a great place for a powerful quote. Oh, well."*
> —Eugene Mirman

> *"And so would this."*
> —Eugene Mirman

Peer Counselor FAQ (Not Literally)

My career in advice-giving predates my comedy career by many years. From my sophomore to my senior year of high school, I worked at a crisis peer counseling hotline. In order to work the phones, we received months of training about all kinds of topics, from relationships, family issues, depression, sex abuse, drugs, and much more. For instance, here's a quick suicide fact: if someone claims they're suicidal, you *must* ask if they have a plan. Anyone can claim they want to kill themselves (attention-grabber), but there's a completely different level of risk if someone has a plan ("My dad has a gun in the basement," "There are sleeping pills in the bathroom . . ." as opposed to, "I don't know; maybe with food . . . ?"). Don't be afraid to ask if they have a plan; you're not encouraging the idea of suicide to a person that's told you they're suicidal (unless they suffer from a short-term-memory disorder).

Don't get me wrong—though we had crisis training, most of the calls that we received were actually from middle-aged perverts. One chronic caller was locked out of his apartment every night—naked. Another made sex noises. That's life. I actually forget most of the training we received—it was long ago and I was only sixteen anyway. What has stayed with me is a desire to help people, and also, a desire to use humor as a way to hide from *and* engage the pain of the world.

A comedian is simply a different kind of therapist. A comedian is a psychologist and a psychiatrist rolled into one. Except I can't prescribe medicine. (You still need a doctorate, which is bullshit.) Okay, so I'm not like a psychiatrist. Fine. But I'm still like a psychologist (except I can't diagnose or treat mental illness).

But who is my patient? Society. The world. You, me, and

Dupree, and also everyone else. (By the time you are reading this, that movie will be so far from your memory that I should apologize for making you remember it. So, I will. I am truly sorry.)

Your mind (which is very advanced—congratulations!) is racing with questions.

Don't worry, here are the answers:

Who are you?

Fuck you.

Okay. How did the idea for this book come about?

Actually, for the past six years I've been running an advice column on my Web site. People can write me and I answer some questions and post the responses on my site. Over the years I've received thousands of e-mails looking for guidance. Some have real problems; some talk about monkeys and poo—though those people may also have real problems.

Also, I'm always trying to brainstorm about how to make small amounts of money from giant companies—and a book seemed like the perfect idea.

Are you in any way qualified?

Yes? No? It doesn't matter. In America, "Qualification" is simply an attitude. I've adopted it. So, yes. I am qualified.

However, to alleviate any concerns, I plan to buy as many doctorates as I can from online unaccredited universities. Maybe as many as twenty doctorates! So don't worry, I've got more degrees than Bruce Lee! (Although I have never heard someone make that joke, I bet it was done quite a bit at parties in the '70s.)

Did you have a spiritual awakening that inspired your teachings?

Yes. A little.

If I read this and talk about it at parties, will people think I'm great?

Definitely. Aside from imparting my Awesome Knowledge, this book is a simple way to brand yourself as "cool."

Obviously, some things, like movies, newspapers, and music, have had decades to help people define themselves—whether they are intellectuals or tough guys, classy or crass, people align themselves with cultural things that help them define themselves for others at school, on social networking sites, at work, or parties, etc. It starts as a young adult with being metal or Goth or a hippie, but it continues for the rest of your life. Fancy smarty-pants-ies read the *New York Times* or *Wall Street Journal* (except the editorial page—right??!!!), workin' folks read the *Post* and John Grisham (not for news, I hope).

Although I haven't had as much time as Jonathan Swift to create a brand identity for myself, let me just say, if you enjoy and understand my book, it probably means you are smart (possibly brilliant), down to earth, and nice-looking. Plus, you're probably on your way to both wealth of the heart (Love) and wealth of the money (Money).

However, if you do not enjoy/get this book, you are an ignorant, shameful sex offender who was born poor, which at least in the UK means you can never rise above your class. Sorry, that's just the brand identity I've created. You can create one, too. That's right, amongst my myriad teachings you'll learn how to stop thinking of yourself as a person and start thinking of yourself as a brand. Sure, maybe nobody wants to fuck Joe Smith (that's you in this example), but once Joe Smith re-brands himself, nobody will want to keep him out (of their vaginas!). That example works for girls, too, because

I explicitly say that you are Joe Smith in this example. I will try to make my next one from a woman's point of view. For instance, you are Susan Macintyre and everyone wants you to defend them in court. I think that sort of works. Obviously, I have swapped out guys' prurient desire for sexual prowess with women's desire to be the best lawyers they can. But it still works as an analogy.

Chief, just tell us, what really is this Will to Whatevs?

It is a self-explanatory concept that you Will the world you live in, barring any terrible tragedy, like being too fat to go outside, having an airplane fall on you at the mall, or having the misfortune of being born outside of North America, Europe, Japan, or twelve other places.

Is it actually helpful, or a joke by someone who worships irony and cynicism like they're going out of style? (I don't understand that expression, and I apologize if I've used it wrong.)

Oh, it's very helpful. One day, it will replace books like the Hindi Vedas, which is actually not good news.

Are comedians actually very sad inside, because their job is to make people laugh, so it would be very funny if they were sad, because sadness is the opposite of laughter, as I understand it?

It depends, but that is a very good question. In fact, it is so overwhelming that I'll have to answer it in my next book, *Things People Want to Know about Comedians that They Think Are More Interesting than They Are*. In the book I also address the controversy surrounding firemen, who are 65 to 80 percent water.

To give a better idea of who I am, my experiences, and qualifications, here is a timeline of my life.

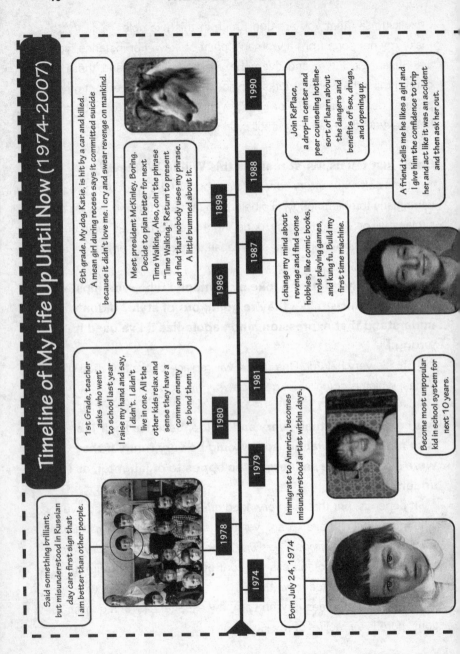

Timeline of My Life Up Until Now (1974-2007)

1974 — Born July 24, 1974

1978 — Said something brilliant, but misunderstood in Russian day care first sign that I am better than other people.

1979 — Immigrate to America, becomes misunderstood artist within days.

1980 — 1st Grade, teacher asks who went to school last year I raise my hand and say, I didn't. I didn't live in one. All the other kids relax and sense they have a common enemy to bond them.

1981 — Become most unpopular kid in school system for next 10 years.

1986 — 6th grade. My dog, Katie, is hit by a car and killed. A mean girl during recess says it committed suicide because it didn't love me. I cry and swear revenge on mankind.

1987 — I change my mind about revenge and find some hobbies, like comic books, role playing games, and kung fu. Build my first time machine.

1898 — Meet president McKinley. Boring. Decide to plan better for next Time Walking. Also, coin the phrase "Time Walking." Return to present and find that nobody uses my phrase. A little bummed about it.

1988 — A friend tells me he likes a girl and I give him the confidence to trip her and act like it was an accident and then ask her out.

1990 — Join RePlace, a drop-in center and peer counseling hotline—sort of learn about the dangers and benefits of sex, drugs, and opening up.

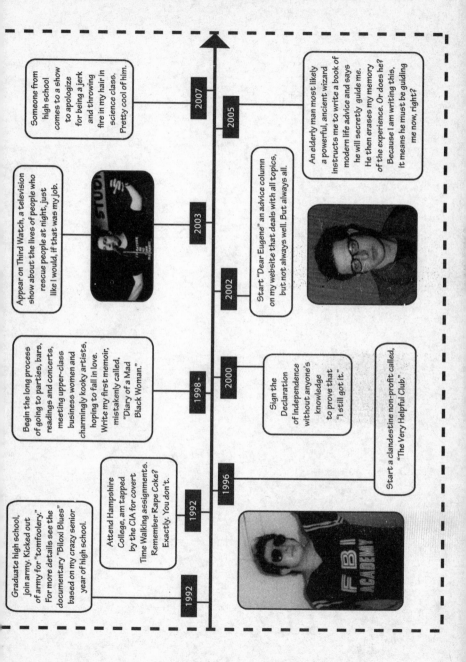

Graduate high school, join army. Kicked out of army for "comfoolery." For more details see the documentary "Biloxi Blues" based on my crazy senior year of high school.

1992

Attend Hampshire College, am tapped by the CIA for covert Time Walking assignments. Remember Rape Coke? Exactly. You don't.

1992

Begin the long process of going to parties, bars, readings and concerts, meeting upper-class business women and charmingly kooky artists, hoping to fall in love. Write my first memoir, mistakenly called, "Diary of a Mad Black Woman."

1998 -

Sign the Declaration of Independence without anyone's knowledge to prove that "I still got it."

2000

1996

Start a clandestine non-profit called, "The Very Helpful Club."

Appear on Third Watch, a television show about the lives of people who rescue people at night, just like I would, if that was my job.

2003

Start "Dear Eugene" an advice column on my website that deals with all topics, but not always well. But always all.

2002

Someone from high school comes to a show to apologize for being a jerk and throwing fire in my hair in science class. Pretty cool of him.

2007

2005

An elderly man most likely a powerful, ancient wizard instructs me to write a book of modern life advice and says he will secretly guide me. He then erases my memory of the experience. Or does he? Because I am writing this, it means he must be guiding me now, right?

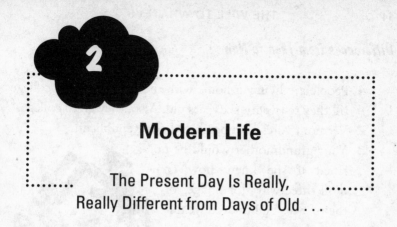

Modern Life

The Present Day Is Really, Really Different from Days of Old . . .

Life is very different now from the way it was over a century ago; just ask any old person. Modern life is full of pressures that our parents, their parents, and previous generations never faced or fathomed. Our grandparents may have had to deal with the Great Depression, but they never had ADHD or Perfectmatch.com to navigate through. Their grandparents may have had twelve-hour workdays in dangerous, filthy factories, and limited medicine, but they can't imagine how hard it is to list your favorite bands on a social networking site in a way that maximizes what strangers think of you. Some of our parents may have gone to college, but did they temp at a weird PR firm or software company? What about the pressure to own an iPod or give a blow job (a term that wasn't even coined until the 1964 Newport Folk Festival!)?

Still not convinced? Wow. Okay. Industry, social codes—so much has evolved or changed, it can sometimes be hard to keep track of it all. You would have to be a robot to list all the changes over the last century (I can't wait!), but here are just a few of the touchstones.

Differences from Then to Now

1. People are living at home with their parents after college till they're twenty-six years old. Also, they go to college.
2. Vermont votes Democrat and not Republican.
3. Your grandmother would be horrified if she knew how common three-ways (or images of them) are. A hundred years ago, if you wanted to see a three-way, you had to look in a card catalogue under Catherine the Great.

4. McDonald's sells salads that make you fat.
5. It is okay for young women to pull up their shirts at parties and scream at each other's breasts, while people record this. (As recently as 1972, guys could only make reel-to-reel audio recordings of girls talking about their ankles.)
6. Homosexuals practice magic out in the open.
7. It is not loathsome to be Japanese (which it was in 1943—fact!).

Homosexuals practicing magic out in the open.

8. LBJ is *dead*! So is Woodrow Wilson.
9. People don't huddle around light bulbs and

Victrolas crying that there is finally a middle class in America.

10. Polio is uncommon.
11. Prostitution is long gone, because most vaginas are naturally full of money (thanks to genetic engineering!).
12. Woman can have jobs—and not just during times of war! Some ladies even make great assistant DAs (if you believe what you see on *Law and Order*).

Daily life has changed a lot over the past 150 years. Typewriters have become computers. Iron stoves have become microwaves. Pegasuses have become helicopters.

But Life's Rule Book hasn't been updated. Many tried—Eisenhower, Carrie Fisher, and John Gray. Even Sigmund Freud gave it a shot with his now forgotten 1942 record of instructional love songs, "I'll Show You How to Do It Without Crying."

Some people think of life as a roller coaster, but you wouldn't have been able to make that analogy very clearly until the mid 1880s (or in France in the 1780s—but you would have thought that life was a Chemin de Centrifuge). Remember early amusement parks? You'd take a girl on the Tea Cup ride, just to "accidentally" brush up against her? Nowadays you can just hold your hand out at a café and a woman will put her breast in it. But if you hold your hand out wrong, she is allowed to stab you. How things have changed.

This timeline better illustrates how times and culture have evolved.

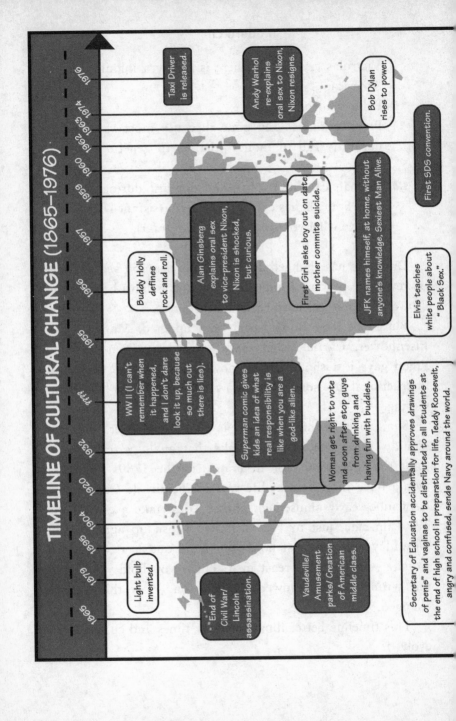

TIMELINE OF CULTURAL CHANGE (1865–1976)

1865 1879 1895 1904 1920 1932 1944 1955 1956 1957 1959 1960 1962 1963 1974 1976

Light bulb invented.

"End of Civil War/ Lincoln assassination.

Vaudeville/ Amusement parks/ Creation of American middle class.

WW II (I can't remember when it happened, and I don't dare look it up, because so much out there is lies).

Superman comic gives kids an idea of what real responsibility is like when you are a god-like alien.

Woman get right to vote and soon after stop guys from drinking and having fun with buddies.

Buddy Holly defines rock and roll.

Alan Ginsberg explains oral sex to vice-president Nixon. Nixon is shocked, but curious.

First Girl asks boy out on date mother commite suicide.

JFK names himself, at home, without anyone's knowledge, Sexiest Man Alive.

Elvis teaches white people about "Black Sex."

First SDS convention.

Taxi Driver is released.

Andy Warhol re-explains oral sex to Nixon, Nixon resigns.

Bob Dylan rises to power.

Secretary of Education accidentally approves drawings of penis" and vaginas to be distributed to all students at the end of high school in preparation for life. Teddy Roosevelt, angry and confused, sends Navy around the world.

TIMELINE OF CULTURAL CHANGE (1980–2014)

1980

Ronald Reagan elected president. Boy George begins work on a "Gay Machine," whatever that is.

1984

Knight Rider and A-Team transform concept of justice for American youth.

1991

E-mail is revealed to non-nerds.

Stills of breasts are available to teens and twenty-somethings. Some teens become promiscuous, but many prefer the immediacy of pornography instead of real sexual encounters. Director of Porky's and Revenge of the Nerds gives up.

1996

2000

Cell phones change business and hooking up forever.

2003

MySpace helps people become famous, provides a safe place for teens to be sexy, and enables older men meet those teens.

Friendster shows you how you know people you don't know.

2004

2005

Youtube gives cats and Japanese cell phone owners a voice.

2007

Presidential election inspires new people who barely understand the world around them to yell at each other in staggering numbers. Hope is restored.

Facebook merges social networking with information and commerce in a way that seems great right now, but we'll see.

2008

2009

2011

Phonetalkerfriend.com makes it possible for cell phones to make friends.

North Korea throws a surprise party for Gene Simmons at the Mall of America, signaling a willingness to repair relations with the United States, and also, a willingness to embrace a new sexual public persona.

2014

Iran attempts to revamp image by recording punk rock covers of Cat Stevens songs (including Where Do the Children Play? and Mona Bone Jakon!). It works a little.

To navigate this crazy new world, you're going to need a guide—someone (I recommend myself) to take your hand and walk you through life. Today's landscape, both literally and figuratively, is changing and evolving (if you believe Al Gore, and also, it is obvious). Think of me as a Life Sherpa, able to breath where most have difficulty, able show a path up the tallest mountain of all—Life Mountain.

Whether you're Buddhist, Christian, Muslim, Jewish, atheist, or agnostic; whether you're one of those hippie kooks who obviously made up his own religion that sort of makes sense, but not really; whether you are an ancient demi-God (not likely, but imagine how much help Hercules would need to simply order a vanilla latte at Starbucks), we could all use assistance. Maybe your dad says that accepting aid is weak—he's right, if the aid is in the form of a check from the government—but he's wrong if it's in the form of advice, guidance, general suggestions, and new ways of looking at things. Then, your dad is just a stubborn asshole. So don't listen to him, listen to me. I'm a modern man, and I have a modern plan. (Note: Manfred Mann, if you are still alive, I just inspired you to write a comeback hit.)

So let's begin life. Let's go to school, fall in love, go dancing, build a rocket ship, solve a crime (not really), start up a start-up, open a fingerprint museum (bad idea, but I'll try to help you if that's what you want), raise a family, and find a political party while having fun at a college kegger. There are too many things to list, but not too many lists to thing. Why? Because you can't "thing" a "list." I bet you did not know that. Anyway, put on your mind-wings and let's go for a fly. . .

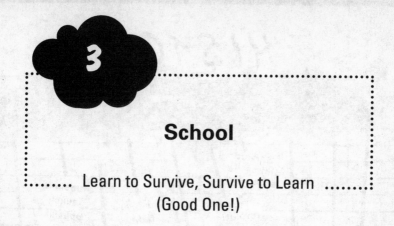

School

Learn to Survive, Survive to Learn
(Good One!)

From birth, people need guidance. At first, all that's asked of a child is to eat mushy food and learn to poop in a specific place that is not on their person. However, nowadays in America, it's basically time for school as soon as humans are able to process language and ideas and form audible words—from regular kids who can say "banana" to Superbabies who can handle the more complicated concept of Schrödinger's Cat.

In New York City, WASPs, Jews, and an increasing number of Indians battle to get their children into the "right" pre-schools so that they can get into Harvard—where they are assigned a part of the world to rule over with a magic ring powered by alien technology. (You don't really need to look further than the number of U.S. presidents and vice presidents who attended or were friends with Harvard alumni to know I am telling the truth.)

Where did all this begin? How did we go from cavemen and women to space travelers, restaurateurs, and lobbyists? The history of education is actually quite interesting, I am told. Because we're all a product of the MTV generation, I've distilled

HISTORY

Beginning

5000 BCE

3000 BCE

Sept. 8, 1636

1789-99

1835

1918

1944

1957

1958

Harvard University is founded.

French revolution' gives world "something to learn about."

The first fight between jocks and nerds breaks out in Springfield, IL.

Russians launch Sputnik into space.

Hieroglyphics help early Egyptians explain cats and sex to one another.

U.S. Senate introduces G.I. bill allowing countless baby boomers to rise in social class, financial standing, and desirability.

The National Defense Education Act (NDEA) passed under President Eisenhower promotes math and science in school. This spells the begin- ing of the end (I made that expression up and sent it back in time- just a cool fact about me) for The Soviet Union and communism.

China and Rome unveil oral teaching traditions in order to keep track of how wrong they are about stuff.

Colthe first American private school opens in New York City to the delight of Dutch settlers. The school was actually founded in 1628, but that would fall too close to Harvard for my timeline, so I moved it. I think you're now getting a glimpse of my true power.

Somewhere between 2.5 million BCE and 5000 BCE (depending on which origin of mankind you believe)—Adam and Eve eat an apple and learn a lesson about disobeying God. This is the last time a human does something a snake suggests.

OF EDUCATION

1984 1991 1998 2001 2007 2009 2012

Theodore Sizer introduces the Coalition of Essential Schools, whatever that is.

No Child Left Behind fixes America's school system. First "Entire World Clap-A-Thon" celebrating U.S. policy held, with entire world actually clapping.

A new postulate is added to mathematics stating that now Y= Y+1. This throws everything off, especially how to build houses.

The movie Toy Soldiers is released showing America that private school fuck-ups can fight terrorists, given the opportunity. Louis Gosset Jr. is helpful and tough.

Harper's magazine has article about how it's not fair to blame U.S. education system for everything. At least that is what is implied in the first few pages and the cover. Who knows what the whole article is about? I have a short attention span, because I was in special ed for six years. However, I was never diagnosed with a disability, so all I know is it's hard for me to read and stay focused. I don't know why. Oh well, those are the pies we have. That is a real Russian saying, enjoy!)

Backdoor sex becomes a popular "safer" form of sex among young teens. Could you imagine how disappointed in America George Washington would be today? I bet even Dorothy Parker would be shocked!

Komputers for Kids, an international non-profit meant to provide kids with laptops, turns out to be a high-end prostitution ring that services only Ban Ki-Moon.

the history of education to just the essential peaks to give you an idea of how we all got here, and how you can get where we're going.

K Through 12

....

Oh, boy. The experience you have here will make a boy into a man, a man-boy into a girl, a girl into a woman, and turn an emotionally unstable tween into a powerful killing machine. School shapes who you become, and most of life is spent reliving it or undoing it, depending on what happened to you and how much cash you have.

At school anyone can be a friend or foe—kids, teachers, administrators, overweight know-it-all Goths, nerds, druggies, preppies (i.e. smart jocks), etc. For twelve years you are basically engaged in a really fun cold war—full of information, secrets, torture, power struggles, espionage, an arms race (literally), hostages (the constant swapping of BFFs), and the occasional skirmish. Sometimes, if things get bad, this good-time cold war can become a bad-time war-war. Good news, some wars end in peace, power, and a greater understanding of the world. Yours can.

If you're lucky, you will spend most of your education peacefully, studying, hanging out, going to Circuit City, or kayaking with friends—far, far away from the fatwas of cheerleaders. Still, for some kids, school can be twelve years of 'Nam—if you thought the Viet Cong were trouble, you've never felt the wrath of a fourteen-year-old girl uncomfortable with the changes in her body, wanting to destroy all she sees.

And for the super unlucky—i.e., the ugly (even moms are

subconsciously more distant from ugly babies), weird, super smart, stinky, foreign, or genuinely annoying—it's your first day of kindergarten and you're Abu Musab al-Zarqawi, and the other kids can tell that you're different, and some even already suspect that you are a wanted Jordanian terrorist.

I'm not saying this to scare you, but to prepare you. It's something I say a lot. It's even in my book *Favorite Rhymey Sayings*, see?

> **"Prepare, don't scare."**
> —Eugene Mirman, from the book
> *Favorite Rhymey Sayings*

However, there's much you can do to enjoy yourself, learn a lot, and become a successful and happy child and young adult. It is far from hopeless—however, you do have to *Will* it.

Elementary School

If you're good at sports and stuff like that, you're all set for the next six years. Being able to run, jump, and throw better than other kids are the most important skills a child can have. The second-most important, although it's not a skill, is to be bigger than other kids, or attractive.

If you're none of these things, you can either just keep to yourself, or impress, bribe, and intimidate the kids in your class. Feel free to experiment with different options. Maybe every Friday of first grade you bring your classmates peanut butter-and-jelly sandwiches? Or maybe it's the last day of fourth grade and you rent a limo and take all the popular kids to a forest and get a giant tattooed guy to make them strip and jump into a freezing pond. They won't say a word to anyone and no one will fuck with you, ever.

If things go well, you'll be invited to sleepovers and everything will be okay. Sadly, *Homo sapiens* younglings (unlike whale babies) act like little, savage politicians.

The most important thing in elementary school, aside from learning basic reading, math, science, and history, is to not leave showing any signs of sociopathy. Try to have fun, make friends, and play games.

Junior High

. . . .

Don't do weird stuff at parties. Just make it out of eighth grade without doing something so embarrassing you get a nickname that implies you shat yourself in class.

High School

. . . .

Oh, man. This is where boys and girls go from tweens to teens and become complicated and cruel. Girls play sick mind games; boys try to pull each other's penises off and throw them in the bushes. If you can, buy the most expensive jeans in a two-hundred-mile radius of your town and wear them on your first day. If anyone asks how you could afford them, say that your father is the president of Ashton Kutcher. When they are like, "Ashton Kutcher has a president?" answer, "Yes." Everyone will be in awe of you and you won't have to go through a lot of pain and cat fights.

Getting Straight A's
· ·

There are three ways to get straight A's (not counting being
so smart that everything comes easily to you). One is to study
hard, do your work as well as you can, and then when you feel
like you can't do any more, do a little more.

The second is to pay someone to do your work, preferably a
wise old man with lots of free time (about sixteen years, if you
intend to go to college). The final way to excel in school is to
get held back or stay in lower-level classes. The extreme version
of option three is to feign full-out retardation and blow people's
expectations away at the age of fourteen. There is nothing more
powerful than pretending for close to a decade that you can
barely comprehend the written word, have terrible math skills,
and can't read social cues, and then one year after you would
have had your Bar Mitzvah—*bam!*—you're witty and good at
earth science!

> *"If no one figures out you are pretending to be retarded, your
> life will be greeted with treasure."*
>
> —Eugene Mirman, from his book
> *Inspirational Proverbs for No One in Particular*

Academics
Math, Social Studies, English, and Science
· ·

To use an old expression, these classes are the "meat and po-
tatoes" of education. If your mind was a mouth, these classes
would be the main course. If math equations were sandwiches
and the Civil War was lamb vindaloo, you would put those

things in your head the way you put food in your mouth. Let me give you another example. Do you know what a chicken cordon bleu is? Well, say instead of ham and cheese rolled inside a butterflied chicken breast, there was everything you could know about the Magna Carta. Once you chewed it up with your mind-teeth and used the toilet at a party, whoever used the bathroom next would understand this seminal legal document that inspired the Beastie Boys song "(You Gotta) Fight for Your Right (to Party)." (This is technically true.)

Like food food, education is the "knowledge food" for understanding. The more you understand, the more power and access you'll have to Life's Overseas Bank Account, where countless treasures—stolen from Jews, or earned honestly—await.

Whether you learn these subjects at school (slightly more convenient) or from very, very high-concept pornography, you'll need to grasp these basic fundamentals. It's simply important.

You may ask yourself, "When will I need to know this?" And it turns out, very often. Many of the things they teach you in high school form the building blocks of the things you'll say at work or drunk at a party for the rest of your life.

Once, during a small dinner party at my parent's house, a friend of theirs asked me, if I could go back to high school and do it over, would I try harder to get better grades? (I graduated with a 2.1 GPA and was a generally terrible student.) I thought about it for a bit, and said, "No." Now, almost ten years later, I'd like to change my answer to, "Not really, because I don't care about grades, but I wish I'd remembered more of what I learned, because knowledge is power, which is why I would never fight Wal-Mart's database."

One of my only real educational regrets was not paying close enough attention to China's post–World War II revolution that solidified its communist standing. Because of my ignorance, I am doomed to repeat China's mistakes.

So the moral is, try hard to remember stuff from high school—it's important. Don't repeat my and Einstein's (yes!) mistake of not doing well in school. But definitely, if you have the chance, do what Einstein did (but I didn't, which is a bummer) after high school, which is blow the world away with genius scientific breakthroughs. Imagine how much of a head start you'll have on that egghead if you do well in school? Right? Go for it.

Electives
Drama, Foreign Language, Home Ec, Art
....

This is where you can cut loose and be yourself. Though parents don't take these classes seriously, they can be even more important than required curriculum. Everybody who's anybody knows that Vassar looks at your home ec grade before deciding whether to let you in. The same is true for Wesleyan and Stamford—not to be confused with Stanford University, in Palo Alto, but the crappy town in Connecticut. Even this boring haven for businesses won't let you in unless you can bake a good cherry pie.

Sex Ed
....

Grownups use this class to scare teens about their bodies. Most of what you are told, often by gym teachers, is half-truths and misinformation. This part is true: Boys have penises and girls have vaginas. If they touch at the wrong time, you can make a baby or die. Even though I have now taught you everything you need to know, you still have to take this class. Sorry.

Your main objective should be to avoid eye contact with the instructors. Anything else you need to know about sex you can Google or read in *Cosmo Girl*, *Time Out* (New York), or *Uncanny X-Men*.

The only thing the instructors teach that you won't find on-line is to be careful using drugs and alcohol. It's one thing to get drunk and hook up with an ugly person when you're twenty-seven, but if you're sixteen, it could make you unpopular.

Extracurricular Activities and After-School Clubs
······································

Joining or creating an after-school club can be a fun way to make friends and explore your interests. You can join a sports team, the chess club, band (if you're a jerk), a pro-life group (oh, boy), a peer leadership group (college kiss-ass), a vague multi-cultural group, or even some sort of edgy art collective like the You-Don't-Get-Us Painters. Either way, have fun with it.

You will most likely encounter lots of bullshit rules about not taking unsupervised field trips. If you're in seventh grade or older, just tell them that you're all young adults and you won't try drugs. If you're younger, it really is a bad idea for a group of preteens to take a bus alone somewhere (unless one of you is magic). Generally, a magic child is special and what he wants to do can save the world.

When you're joining a club, you have to ask yourself three questions:

1. What do I enjoy?
2. Who do I enjoy doing it with?
3. What do I want out of this?

Most likely you either want to make friends, boost your college application, escape an abusive home life, or you really love math and want to do it at night and on weekends with your first- and second-generation immigrant friends (and two white kids whose parents put *Dead Poets Society* pressure on them).

If you join a club to meet a boy or girl, be careful. I once heard of a kid, who was me, who went on a pro-life march in high school, not totally understanding what I was doing, because I had a crush on a girl. I wasn't so retarded (it isn't offensive to use this word if you really mean it) that I joined the club, but still, don't repeat the weird thing I did—let my lesson be yours.

Gym
......

This can be a really fun time to show off your hand-eye coordination and general physical prowess. Sadly, many of the games you'll learn here you will never play again, unless you are cast in a movie about these games.

Gym is also where most people experience showering in groups for the first time. For many, this can be very uncomfortable. If it bothers you, one easy solution is to rent a nearby hotel room and shower there.

Like any specific space, the locker room has its own rules of appropriate behavior. No one will tell you them, but they're good to know.

Locker Room Rules for Boys

1. No horseplay.
2. No riddles (giving or solving).
3. If you do an impression of a teacher, try to make it a fat teacher with a silly voice.
4. If someone insults you, strike him in the throat with a broom.
5. Never set up a kissing booth.

If someone insults you, strike him in the throat with a broom.

No riddles (giving or solving).

Locker Room Rules for Girls

1. No spitting.
2. If you make eye contact with a girl you don't know, look away quickly. Most young girls see eye contact as a form of confrontation. If it's too late, and the girl goes, "What're you looking at?" Say, "Nothing." If she then says something obnoxious, you have my permission to hit her in the throat (with a broom!). Then go, "I just President Bushed you, bitch!"
3. Never tell anyone an embarrassing secret.
4. If you have any kind of meta-human ability (telekinesis, flight, laser-hands), hide it. Teen girls are cruel and will make fun of your gift.
5. Try to act like a lady and say please and thank you before using the toilet.

Never tell anyone an embarrassing secret.

If you have any kind of meta-human ability—i.e., telekinesis, flight, laser-hands—hide it. Teen girls are cruel and will make fun of your gift.

Peer Pressure

· · · · · · · · · · · · · · · · · · ·

This is a big one, folks. If you're the victim of particularly ill-guided peer pressure, it could ruin your life—you could get pregnant, become addicted to dope, get into a terrible car accident (where you break your mustache, maybe worse), or join the Army. An important note: Joining the Army is not a bad thing, just like getting pregnant is not a bad thing—however, both become bad choices if done out of peer pressure, e.g., "Come on, join the Army or get pregnant. It'll be awesome! Everyone is doing it!" Obviously, only a total doofus would join the Army *to* get pregnant. So don't—even if suave 1970s John Travolta suggests it.

You need to develop defenses and give yourself the confidence to say yes or no on your own terms. One way to avoid being the victim of peer pressure is, every morning, to look in a mirror and say to yourself:

I grant myself the gift of personal cool, and no one I idolize, fear, or want to make out with can take that away from me by insisting I smoke dope or something else I don't want to do, including kill an animal, double-team a horny parent, or burn down an abandoned warehouse.

If that's a bit long winded, then just yell, "I'm the tops!"

Again, it's okay to experiment

with alcohol, drugs, violence, and sex in a safe way—but it is not okay to do something because a bunch of teens make you too uncomfortable to say no. Real friends will admire your resolve.

Secret aside to parents: The most common advice mistake that parents make (mid-sentence poem—cool!) of having their kids stand up to peer pressure is to condescendingly evoke the Brooklyn Bridge scenario. The old, "If blankety-blank jumped off the Brooklyn Bridge, would you?" Nothing is actually like that and it just makes kids so mad they turn to hard drugs. Both Bob Dylan and Lou Reed cite their parents saying that sarcastically as the main reason they left home. There is only one situation analogous to it, which is if someone your child admired actually jumped off the Manhattan Bridge and your child was considering doing it, too. The two bridges are very similar and less than a mile apart. You'd be idiots to not take this once-in-a-lifetime opportunity to sarcastically (and ironically!) jab your stupid child.

Quick Peer Pressure Survival Rules

1. Never give in to peer pressure, especially if the peer is not attractive.
2. See rule two.
3. I'm glad you moved on and didn't listen to me. Congratulations. You pass.

Cliquety Cliques
....

Cliques are a big part of high school. They will shape who you become and determine where you are in the social strata of your school. Are you a jock, nerd, preppy, band member, drama geek (and eventual movie star or gay rights activist—hahahahaha, right?), punk rocker, Goth, ho-ho, Canadian (again—haha!), boingy-dong-don, a tough hoodlum, tranny, MILF (not likely), or popular chameleon-esque über-youth?

You need to figure out:

1. What clique are you in?
2. What clique do you want to be in?

For instance, I was in a nerdy clique (sur-fucking-prise!) even though I was "academically challenged"—that's what Democrats are calling it now. I belonged in this group because I liked spaceships, computers, robots, Jethro Tull, and girls at a distance. I didn't want to play lacrosse, because I feared (1) running around with a stick and (2) witnessing sex crimes. Instead, I wanted to see *Star Trek IV: The Voyage Home* (my favorite).

The good news is that by senior year many of the clique walls dissolve and your whole class becomes a Dionysian love-fest. However, before that (or possibly never) you are living in an '80s teen comedy. Most likely, you are the awkward protagonist. Everybody feels like they are an underdog, whether it's true or not—just look at Dane Cook (not straight at him; it would be blinding).

There are four things that go into figuring out what clique to join:

1. How strong are you?
2. How smart are you?
3. How attractive are you?
4. What music do you like?

Game!

Match the description of the person with the clique. Added bonus! No cliques listed, so match them in your head and find out what stereotypes you have!

Fat girl who loves the Doors and is a good photographer.

Football player who is so stupid he catches fire all the time and listens to jazz because someone told him he has to.

A pretty girl who wears glasses and thinks they make her look ugly when they don't at all.

An Indian boy who loves chocolate and does not believe the Holocaust happened.

A Catholic girl who cuts herself, sleeps around, and drinks tea.

A metalhead who gets hard whenever he watches the Discovery Channel show *Dirty Jobs* with Mike Rowe.

A super rich lady Minotaur who is a science wiz. She can also fly!

A strong, slightly slow Jewish boy whose only friend is a train set.

A football player who is so stupid he catches fire all the time and listens to jazz because someone told him he has to.

A super-rich lady Minotaur who is a science wiz.
She can also fly!

A strong, slightly slow Jewish boy
whose only friend is a train set.

> "*I miss the innocence I've known, playing KISS covers beautiful and stoned.*"
>
> —Eugene Mirman, from his album
> *Yankee Hotel Foxtrot* (later popularized by Wilco)

Different combinations of these things determine who your friends will be. If you're very smart and listen to emo, but you are ugly, your friends will be fringe Goths. However, if you like emo and are strong and somewhat smart, you might be friends with bisexual soccer players (or even be one of them!). See how this works?

Defeating a Bully

Most bullies are the product of a stressful and often abusive home life. Next time a bully threatens or attacks you, just yell, "Don't abuse me like your parents abuse you!" Then call children's services and tell them you saw this bully crying in the bathroom and you're worried about him. Bam! He just got moved to a foster home.

Prom
Not a Big Deal, but Try and 69 If You Can

Prom night can be a special night, if you let it be. I know you think it's for losers and something that popular kids do because they are boring people with porcelain hearts who don't know what it means to be lonely. But you're wrong. Prom is a chance for everyone to try oral sex. Go for it. Make sure you have at least one beer (no more than four, though). Where can you get liquor? You must have a friend who has "cool" parents; have them get you some. Okay?

Right College, Wrong Other Thing

....

You already know that it's important to get the best grades you can. You know to do lots of well-rounded, extra curricular activities, and if you took my and your guidance counselor's advice, you joined some clubs that make you look good. And I'm sure you kicked ass on your SATs! So congrats, Mr. and Mrs. Good At Standardized Tests.

However, in today's ultracompetitive college admission process, there is nothing better than doing something above and beyond to standout to admissions people. A good way to get into any college (except Notre Dame) is to develop an HIV vaccine. Any teen who has the balls to cure AIDS would be a highly sought-after freshman. There is also a 98 percent chance Bono would call and thank you.

The other thing you can do is write a strong personal essay which lets admissions people inside your life, your heart, and your world. Though getting to know you is the reason colleges require personal essays now, originally the concept was started by Harvard to prevent so many Jews from getting in, because immigrants are sneaky—you couldn't tell who was Jewish by their last name, but you could from an essay titled, "My First Shabbat." Anyway, it can be hard to figure out what to write about, so here are a few suggestions:

1. How old people and young people are the same in so many ways, except age.
2. A concert or reading you went to that had a powerful affect on you.
3. How you overcame adversity (and tricking someone slightly older into having sex does not count).

4. How people are animals, but shouldn't be hunted.
5. Reasons it's wrong to be racist even though it makes sense to you.
6. Pearl Jam.
7. How your parents met their new spouses.
8. The perfect murder.
9. Your favorite places to throw up.
10. An essay titled, "If I Were Eric Clapton . . ."

College
....

College is basically a repeat of junior high. So just remember: Don't do weird stuff at parties and make it out of there without doing something so embarrassing you get a nickname that implies you shat yourself in class.

Oh, I almost forgot! Don't be too smug and arrogantly vocal about your world views—it can ruin lunch. You know what? I think this would be simpler if I just revealed . . .

The Five Golden Rules of College

1. Learn something you either really enjoy or will make you rich, but not something your parents insist is a smart career. They probably still think Google is short for googolplex—a very, very large number.
2. It is okay to fight to legalize pot, but don't do it while wearing a silly hat *and* skirt if you're a guy, or something knitted out of leaves and beads if you're a lady.
3. *Do not* videotape yourself having sex with porn stars

(or anyone) at a frat party, even if it's to raise money for Habitat for Humanity.

4. Buddhism and communism are goofy ideas invented by foreigners, so take them with a grain of salt.

5. If you hook up with a professor, keep a diary so your kids will know the naughty you. (This is a fake rule, meant to keep you on your toes. Stay savvy and you won't get Alzheimer's.)

The Fifty N's of Nightlife

Parties, Prostitutes, Bar Crawls (Never Do One), Booty Texts, and Mostly Other Stuff, Which Is a Lot

The Night

Since 1928, people have been asking the same question: *How do I make the Night my own?* Or, *how do I Own the Night?*

First, you need a Corvette. That's not true. That's what a rooky Night Owner would think. You don't need a 'Vette. You don't need a lot of money, although it helps. A common misconception of money is that money can't buy you love. That's true. But money can lead to a series of misunderstandings that can *afford* you love. Think of that last thing as a quick bonus lesson from another dimension.

One of the first times I went on an official date-date, which I know no one does anymore (except Wall Street douche bags and Wiccans), was incredibly awkward. It was just after college and I asked out a pretty girl who worked at a Web design company with a friend of mine. (She also did part-time modeling!) It was the mid-'90s and most of my Nightlife experience involved sharing inexpensive whiskey at home with friends, doing weird comedy shows, going to a few concerts, and having many late-night debates about the ultimate Truth of the universe. Hers involved going to dance clubs and fancy parties with low-level sheiks. I probably had about eighty dollars in my checking account. (I worked at an ice cream parlor.) We went to a dance club and it was a twenty-dollar cover! What the fuck? Twenty dollars! For what? There's no band or anything. Twenty dollars to get into Shitbag City. (That was the actual name of the club.) Before that I'd never paid a cover to just be inside a place.

In hindsight, I realize that twenty dollars is a very fair price for law students, executive administrative assistants, project managers, COOs, and lonely Europeans to pay for the chance to drink martinis, groove to an overwhelming audio pounding—like a million techno dicks slapping you from all sides—and yell personal details to semi-attractive strangers. This is before date-rape drugs were in, so there was nothing to fear at clubs (except possibly marrying an asshole).

At some point I asked her if I could get her a drink in such an awkward way that she asked me if I was pretending to be uncomfortable. I wasn't. I'd never been to a dance club or gone on a date-date and I felt socially anxious and super awkward. That's what I get for going to an alternative hippie college that questioned gender roles all the time. Still, I learned two important things from that night (about the Night):

1. I do not like going to dance clubs, especially in downtown Beantown.
2. The Night is a dangerous, complicated lion-lady that if tamed can bring bliss—but if misunderstood can lead to self-destruction (à la David Crosby, everyone in *Less Than Zero*, the folks at Studio 54, Alan Thicke, etc.).

To understand the Night, we must ask some questions. Then you must do a shot. Then you should run outside, yell something silly at a stranger (like, "Help! Fart police! Coming through!"), run back in, and put on some nice clothes—because it's almost time to go out for the Night. (If you are in a suburban area and there are no people in the streets, after doing the shot, call information and say something crazy-goofy to the operator. BTW—if you're interested in making an unsuccessful romantic comedy, call it *Crazy-Goofy*.)

Frequently Asked Night Questions

What is the Night?

It is when the sun goes down and the fun comes up.

What is this Night Owner's Code that you haven't mentioned?

There are two basic rules to it: Try not to do anything that makes you want to hire a prostitute to "help you hide from the pain," and do not do anything that would make you want to become a prostitute. Also, no swords, duh!

How late does the Night go?

The Night can go from 5:00 p.m. to as late as 9:00 or 10:00 a.m. After 10:00 a.m., most likely you are not staying up late and connecting with someone, but either rambling about something boring from your past or watching an action-porn you bought at a pharmacy.

Are Day Walkers and Night Owners enemies?

No. Not at all. Both can live in harmony. The main thing to keep in mind is to not talk on your cell phone loudly. You will seem like an asshole at any time. However, the two may have trouble raising a family, unless that family is high all the time and loves to party, but also enjoys school and going for a run.

Safety Rules: The Night Is Not a Toy

Sir Isaac Newton, or the first certified tranny, as he will be known once you add that to Wikipedia (please do it), noticed about the physical world around us, "For every action there is an equal and opposite reaction." Good job, Newts.

A similar but ultimately pretty different rule can be applied to the Night: "For how much fun you can have, there is an equal amount of danger potential." That isn't totally true. Each time you go to a bar, a baby doesn't die. But each time a baby dies, you happen to be at a bar. Go figure?

If you follow the Night's safety rules they can protect you and keep trouble at bay. Obviously, nothing can safeguard you from freak events—insane meth-heads in a helicopter bent on eating you, a privileged twenty-five-foot banker with a pair of sai who lusts to ruin your bachelorette party, or simply a dope fiend needing one more fix. (That last example I borrowed from a 1950s pamphlet promoting fear.)

However, you can do lots of things to stay safe. There are more than two dozen ways to avoid meeting a douche bag with a pocket full of Rohypnol and a conscience the size of a kitten's ding-dong. How do you tell the difference between an awesome, slightly dangerous party, and a party full of coked-up thugs (and not the sexy kind that mom wouldn't like, the unsexy kind that smell like wet socks)?

Here are some basic guidelines for staying safe at night. I am dividing the suggestions by gender, partially out of convenience, and partially to infuriate John Stoltenberg (author of *Refusing to Be a Man*) and his cabal of feminazi cronies.

For Ladies

....

1. Always bring a friend, and keep tabs on each other.
2. Do not eat a sandwich if the person who gave it to you is laughing and clapping.
3. Do not go into a building that has been abandoned for years.
4. Wear thick steel underwear. Obviously, it is not your fault if you are attacked, but sexual predators shut down when they see thick steel underwear. And carry a dildo with mace in it!
5. Before going home with a guy, give him a blow job. Guys are always more relaxed after a blow job. (You're totally welcome, guys. P.S. Girls can't see this sentence!!!!!)
6. Train in several martial arts styles, especially in Krav Maga (Israeli Army "no-nonsense" method), kendo (bamboo swords), and jujitsu (all around ass-kicking).
7. If you are at a party with more than five people named Chad, get the fuck out right away.
8. Do not mouth off to a lunatic wearing a helmet.
9. Throw up on anyone who gives you the creeps.
10. Never make eye contact with a bi-curious designer—she's trouble.
11. If you take a stranger home and have sex with them, videotape it so that if he or she (pretty cool how non-judgmental I am, huh?) does something weird, you will

have proof. Wait a second. Do not have sex with strangers, unless you know them from television.

Do not eat a sandwich if the person who gave it to you is laughing and clapping.

Throw up on anyone who gives you the creeps.

For Gentlemen

1. Do not yell at people bigger than you, especially if you are drunk and wrong.
2. If you have sex with a girl, make sure to use protection, otherwise she will get pregnant, keep the baby, and try to marry you. I'm kidding, but not enough.
3. Never enter a physical contest with someone who acts like a superhero or has silly clothes.
4. When walking late at night, pretend you're fighting an invisible sailor and talk to yourself.
5. Wear a glove with claws on it.
6. Never drink something you find on the street.
7. Don't go to a bar that is on fire.
8. Try not to be tough around people who have been in jail for a long time.

9. Do not make an "oink" sound around a police officer. Or a fart noise around a priest.
10. Never accept a gift from a homeless person, even if they claim to be a wizard, warlock, or a Democrat! (Fake joke alert!)

When walking late at night, pretend you're fighting an invisible sailor and talk to yourself.

Never accept a gift from a homeless person, even if they claim to be a wizard, warlock, or a Democrat! (Fake joke alert!)

Going Out

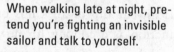

Bar Etiquette: The Secret Code

Going to a bar is like playing a sexy game of chess, or a slightly drunk, low-stakes game of rugby. I think you know what I mean (and if not, please pretend to; it will be easier for both of us). Whether you're the king or queen playing to win, or just a bunch of knights, rooks, and forwards (that's a real position in rugby!!!) looking to fool around, the bar is a "zone" full of delicate nuances that need to be strictly adhered to. Can

you fuck someone in the bathroom? Not without taking appropriate steps first. Can you come up to someone while wearing
a panda costume and ask them silly questions about Chairman
Mao? Yes. Actually, that you can do. I used to do it all the time
circa-2003 in Brooklyn. But you need a permission slip. From
who? First, your own balls. (Balls are just like guts, but much
more street. The term applies to men and women and should
not be taken as a patriarchal jab that women should be paid
less in the workplace, which they should not—unless their job
is to pee standing up—then it would be completely unfair to
pay women as much as men.) Second, you must adopt an inter-
nal compass that leads you through the etiquette of the kind of
bar you're in.

Dive Bar

Dive bars are the classic American bar full of all kinds of
people. In large cities they can function as a conduit for new
schools of thought in technology, philosophy, art, and music
(which is the most "real" form of art, if you believe Schopenhauer). All types of hooligans can be found at dive bars—
naughty art students, elderly divas, atheists, others, writers,
rockers, trannies, regular folk, myself, two black people, and
gun slingers (the last one is true only pre-1890).

It's a great place to unwind, but in some instances people
will want to fight you. That's very rare. I have been to dive bars
in more than fifty cities and you would have to be a real dick
for that to happen. Just don't wear your "Hahvad" sweatshirt,
chucklehead. (I just saw Toby Keith use that word on television—so it's real.) I know this is unfair, since Harvard is a very
good school. And I know when asked where you went to school,
you first say "Massachusetts," then you say "Cambridge," and

finally you begrudgingly admit to being one of the smartest people in your age group. Anyway, have fun. Mix it up.

Sports Bar

A great place to catch a game and hang out with buddies. Other than FOX Sports Grill, which seems unnecessary, most sports bars, like Packard's and Fitzwilly's, are about appetizers and sports.

In many advice books for women, authors suggest that women go to sports bars to meet men. So, if you are a woman, do that. If you are a man and you see a pretty women, club her on the head and tell her she's pretty (*only* at a sports bar).

Sports bars are also a great place for guys to meet other guys—either for sex or for wrestling, whichever feels more right. However, because some men find the advances of other men upsetting, you need to understand the subtleties of picking up guys in potentially hostile environments.

When you first walk into a sports bar, scope it out. Get a feel for the place. Then raise both your arms and yell, "I'm a gay dude looking to party!" Then motion your head towards the bathroom and shout, "Who wants to play Senator?"

Half the dudes will think you're kidding, and the other half will take your brashness as an E-vite to your ding-ding™. Congrats, bro!

Pleasant Fancy Bar

This is a place where nice people go to talk about their marriages or catch up about college. Feel free to try the ceviche, but I recommend the charcuterie plate. There are also lots of business people talking about how much money they'd like to make off of new ideas. Find a group of suits and pitch your new idea. If they are recently divorced, take advantage of them. I'm kidding. Or am I? (If they have kids, please be gentle when you screw them over.)

Shit-Bag Money Jerk Fancy Wannabe Bar

This bar is full of assholes. It's fancy, but in all the wrong ways. Like it was designed by a wolf who won ten million dollars. Feel free to come up to someone and yell, "Make me rich!" Then slap them and go somewhere else. However, do try the seafood tower; it may be very good.

Bar for Indian People

I made this bar up. I am sure that in predominantly Indian areas (like Nagpur, India) they are common, but this isn't a type of bar. I will be "pushing the envelope" (an expression coined by Calvin Coolidge's top-secret homosexual Japanese slave) throughout this book to help you question your cultural assumptions through lies and misdirection. Look over there. See?

Fake Cool Bar

This bar has some kind of affectation that doesn't work. If it's the only place around and you want to catch up with friends, go ahead, of course. Never sacrifice too much comfort or ease for style.

How can you tell if you're in a fake cool bar? Is there a velvet rope? Almost every place (except the airport or a bank) that uses a velvet rope sucks.

However, if there are other options, tap whoever you'd like to talk to and say, "Come with me," in a I'm-from-the-future-and-have-a-warning way and go to a more pleasant place.

Actually Pretty Cool Bar

This is a nice place. It's probably got a great jukebox and a charming staff. It's a lovely place to hang out, meet people, or play Scrabble. Most of the folks there are either great, fucked up in a pleasantly interesting way, or boring, but not dangerous. Like anywhere in the world, there may be a few assholes. But this is often the best place to hang out.

Gay or Lesbian Bar

If you're in here you probably know what to do. A smile goes a long way, so no need to dress too provocatively. I have just a few warnings—do not take crystal meth to heighten your sexual experience. It will lead to a life unwanted and a body wasted. You don't need poppers or whatever.

Clubbing

I recommend not going clubbing. However, if you want to yell at really hot people while shaking around, I understand. The main thing about clubbing is simply getting into the club. It may not be enough to wear Prada pumps to get past the judgmental bouncer with his ivory clipboard. (Most bouncers hunt elephants for their tusks to make their exclusive clipboards—and by clubbing you are contributing to their extinction.)

The best way to get in a club is to become very famous. Celebrities are always treated great at places like that. I was once at a dance club in Las Vegas with some rock stars, and we were all treated very nicely. I even threw ice everywhere and hugged giant men, and no one seemed to mind.

How do you become famous? Well, luckily, you only have to be famous in that one-block radius. You should pay Ozzy Osbourne a million dollars to walk up to you in line, high-five you and go, "Let's go inside and party, my famous friend." If Ozzy won't do it, I'm sure Alan Greenspan would.

Internet fame is also possible. Get out your camera phone, run into the street, light a bunch of smoke bombs in your butt (I know, crass—but effective) and upload that to YouTube (or Revver.com if you want to make cash from it). Come back in thirty minutes and you'll get in.

Rock Concerts: Looking Right, Feeling Wrong
(This Doesn't Mean Anything as Much as It Sounds Good)

Wear something comfortable, but cool. Never look like you are trying to join the band. *Important tip for girls:* Unless you are visibly injured, people will try to do it with you. So please, don't wear something too revealing—unless it is part of that band's audience dress code.

Obviously, if you have very low self-esteem, feel free to wear something provocative. I'll understand.

Back Stage: The Ultimate Party

Getting back stage and partying with the band is often the prize of attending a rock concert (except if you see Ralph Nader's band). In 1985, all you'd have to do is lift your shirt and the roadie would let you into some under-stage sex chamber. It's a new century now, and most roadies are more professional and not as impressed by a flash of flesh (great song title?). And though nothing I say will dissuade you from trying to get backstage, know this: Most backstage areas are a little cramped and have people sitting around eating carrots and mediocre cold cuts. There is a 58 percent chance that if you get backstage, you will regret it a little and feel uncomfortable. Not only that, but you will also ruin the illusion of rock and roll for yourself.

Still want to party? Okay, mo-fo. It's on. What to do? Well, it's pretty easy to make a fake press pass. Go to some rock magazine's Web site (*Harp*, *Magnet*, *CMJ*—stay away from *Rolling Stone* and *Time*), swipe the logo, and Photoshop yourself a pass. (*Note:* Reporters don't actually go to concerts with passes from their magazine, but no one will know or care. Come to think of it, just make a fake business card instead.) Another option is to e-mail the record label and try to get on the guest list by pretending to be the mayor or Dennis Hopper (all bands love Dennis Hopper).

Remember: It is easier to get backstage if you plan ahead. If you're already at the show, try befriending one of the opening bands by telling them some bullshit about the universe. Bands love it when fans answer their metaphysical questions. Don't get too drunk, and *never* try the onion dip.

Theater and Opera

I know that these are perfectly valid forms of art. I bet they are both beautiful. Good luck.

Capture the Flag Fuckfest
(Help Make Our Dream Come True)

This is a version of capture the flag that I've just made up—you tackle someone by making out with them. Hopefully this will escalate into a thirty-person fuckfest as the game goes on. I haven't figured out all the rules, but I'm not the one in a frat, you are. So break out some beers and figure the rules out.

Parties
· · · · · · · · · ·

You're invited, but are you going? Love them or hate them, parties are parties. (Is that something a newscaster would say on television? I think so.)

Whether you're two years old or dead, you're probably on your way to a party. America has 65 percent more parties than France and over 550 percent more parties than North Korea! That's because North Korea is terrible.

There are all kinds of parties and each one has different expectations of you, just as you of it (U of IT—sounds like a shitty tech school, right?). Lots of people feel very out of place at parties. This can be true for all walks of life—artists, coked-up cheerleaders, baristas, university professors, office managers, even helicopter pilots and lady priests (ministers?). Everyone sometimes feels like they don't know what to do or say. Here are some different kinds of parties and how to behave at them so that people don't talk about you in a negative or mocking way (like they do now).

House Parties

There are two kinds of house parties—those thrown by people under twenty-five and those thrown by people over twenty-five. The following rules apply to all house parties, except those thrown by potheads. But don't go to a pothead's house party, okay?

High School/GED/College House Party

These parties can either be a really fun time with your friends, or a brutal reminder of how lonely and isolated you are. And it's only at the end of the night that you truly know which party you were at.

You may show up, excited to reveal that you've had a crush on someone for years. But you find them making out in the corner with someone—who you *know* they hate—and who is not as good as you. What the fuck, right? But that is life. And that is a house party.

Maybe you show up right after a fight with your parents. You don't give a fuck about anything and you are brooding and sexy in the corner. Some hot dude or lady—from a totally different clique!!!—comes up to you, offers you a vodka tonic, and you gulp it down. You're both like, "Let's go for a walk." Months later, you are one of the happiest, most together couples at your school—plus you end years of war between Goths and preppies! Nice!

A house party is what you make of it—unless you are a Super-loser. Superlosers need to resort to extreme measures, mostly found in '80s movies (*Better Off Dead*, where an outcast has to beat a jock skiing on one leg; *Weird Science*, where a computer wizard lady helps give teens confidence; *Footloose*, where a crippled young man challenges a town to a dancing contest and wins, etc.). However, barring these extremes, just have a positive outlook and don't wear a stupid shirt, and you should be fine.

To survive, you will need two things: a knife, and a small water bong. I'm kidding—you will need a sense of humor and to eat a big meal beforehand so you don't get too drunk, or if you do, have something cool to throw up (like sesame noodles or braised rabbit). Also, feel free to bring a condom, if you have either low self-esteem in a trashy way, or high "FF" (Fuckfest) self esteem. Good luck, and use common sense to stay out of trouble—i.e., do not get into a Camaro with a drunk to go get another six-pack, okay? There is no need for it.

Post-College-but-Under-Twenty-Five-Year-Old's House Party

Like life, each party starts with a question: What do I want from this? Possible options include: cutting loose, hooking up, making new friends, drunkenly talking about nothing but thinking you are in fact making a wonderful breakthrough, and getting a new job. There are more, but you should discover them on your own.

What should I bring?

It doesn't really matter, but if you want to seem like a hero bring some grapefruits or a six-pack, or cheap rum. If it's a house warming, then you can bring some kind of kitchen thing, like a coffee mug that says Keep It Real or an old pan. They'll love it. The only exception is if the person throwing the party went to an Ivy League college. Then you *have* to bring *Don Quixote* or something wooden from Nantucket with an ancient saying. Trust me, they'll *love* it.

How should I behave?

Do whatever you want. Break stuff, touch your penis or boobs to anything, whatever.

What should I talk about?

If you want to tell a story that you think is funny, you can. But be careful. Some solid topics to stick to that everybody can get in on are former hot teachers, parents, and social justice.

I want to bring my guitar. What songs should I cover?

Don't do it. It is not okay. However, if you must, you can cover the following songs:

1. "Catch the Wind," by Donovan.
2. Any song by Wilco.
3. "Desolation Row," by Bob Dylan.
4. "Hotel California," by whoever did that song. Just kidding, I know it's the Eagles. However, what you don't know is if you write their name three times, they appear. And that's one. Be careful.
5. "New Slang" by the Shins.
6. The entirety of *Fiddler on the Roof.*
7. "Funky Cold Medina."
8. Any pop song you can think of by a Chinese person. (Before you play it, you have to explain that it is your favorite song by a Chinese person, so that people really get excited.)

I get very anxious at parties. Do you know any exercises to cope with crippling social anxiety?

Yes! There are lots of things you can do that will make you feel comfortable around (1) people you like, (2) people you want to like you, and (3) aggravating douche bags.

Nine Steps to Being Comfortable at a Party

1. Have a drink.
2. Everyone knows the old trick of imagining everyone in their underwear. But did you know that if you imagine them crying also, you really will feel better?
3. Go to the bathroom, get in the shower, and tell yourself you're the best!
4. Think of all the things that make you special. (If you can't come up with more than three, you should leave the party right away.)
5. Face Your Fear, Version 1: Give everyone a flower and say, "This is the beginning of our friendship."
6. Face Your Fear, Version 2: If you have a pocket knife, stop the music and yell, "Who wants to be my blood brother?" Then laugh and go, "Only kidding. Conversation about religion in the corner in five minutes."
7. See a therapist or go on medication. It's okay to seek help—it shows that humans are not the arrogant, impulsive beings that aliens will think we are.
8. Take a secret poop in a public place and keep it to yourself.
9. Make a point to say your own name five times to each person you meet.

Over-Twenty-Five-Year-Old's House Party

This party is completely different from the previous one. The rules change. It doesn't matter what your goal is here—because survival must become your goal. Think of everyone at this party as a potential enemy. You *must* destroy them first. How do you do this? Radiation or poison. Bring something deadly. Then, find two allies. Wait a second. I'm sorry. This is only true at a postapocalyptic house party. If the world has not been mangled by a deadly war, then this party still has some different rules from the under-twenty-five-year-old's, but most of the people are not dangerous.

To relax at a party, sit in a corner and cry (this only works for tiny, cute girls—large men, do not try this).

What should I bring?

Wine.

How do I behave?

Like a normal person. You can dance a little if other people are dancing. Do not make loud sounds or knock anything over.

What should I talk about?

This is easy: therapists, bosses, international law, and recipes. The most important thing is to try read an issue of *Harper's* magazine (or commentary) before you go to the party. Feel free to talk about anything you read in there.

The biggest faux pas at these parties is talking about new music. Nobody wants to know about this "new" music and how cool you are at these parties. In fact, the following five subjects should be avoided:

1. Assholes (the place on the body, not people who act like it).
2. Water parks.
3. Animals that sound like people when they make noises.
4. Places to buy inexpensive soap.
5. Things you would have sex with if all people were dead.

High-Society Parties

This party is a complicated affair. The problem is, everyone at this party, with the possible exception of the people throwing it and celebrities, are boring or troubled. However, it is an amazing place to find investors. Once at a party at a multibillionaire's home, I jokingly suggested the idea of a pot that could strain pasta. I think we all know what happened after that. If you're bored, grab your date's hand, go to a nearby wooded area with some peach puree and a bottle of champagne and just talk.

If you decide to stay, try to steal as much stuff as you can. Anyone can steal a fork, but can you steal thirty? Forty? A DVD player? A recumbent bike? This isn't about profit; it's about cunning and the art of setting and accomplishing goals.

Dinner Parties

Two rules: No farting, and smile a lot.

Bachelor/Bachelorette Parties

This is every person's rite of passage—the last time you have fun before you tie the knot. That's what some people would have you believe. But did you know that you are allowed to have fun even after you are married? So take it easy, horny fellas and crazy ladies. I have to say that there is little worse than a bachelorette party. However, if you see a woman wearing an edible penis necklace and she does not have a boyfriend, you just hit a one-night-stand jackpot! Take this "scratch ticket" to a corner store and cash in! What? Never mind.

Five rules: Keep everything a secret, never suck on a stripper's dick (male or female), always tip bartenders, do not go near water (too dangerous), and bring a high-powered air rifle.

Bonfire Ocean Party

This is your chance to hook up with the hunk that you didn't realize liked you. It is also a chance to demonstrate survival skills. Have a beer, jump into the water, punch out the biggest sea creature you find (à la *Beowulf*), and present the trophy to your object of desire. Pheromones will do the rest.

Pajama Parties

Regardless of your age, this is a fun time. If you are under thirteen years old, it is a time to share and play games. If you are eighteen to thirty-four, you can also share and play games. However, be careful; your games may end in a lifetime commitment. If you are over thirty-four and find yourself at a pajama party, you need to ask yourself three questions:

1. Am I very lucky?

2. Am I a criminal in the middle of a crime?

3. Am I a New Age adventurer on a quest?

Once you answer those questions, the right thing to do becomes clear. To help, a few hints: It isn't a pajama party if you drug someone wearing pajamas.

Throwing a Party

Make sure to buy tons o' booze, fries, carrot soup, cheese-cake, duck confit, gorgonzola and pear raviolis, sliders, mayo salad, and anything else you can think of that will (1) impress your guests and (2) maybe make them sick. People need to remember your party—hopefully because they had a super fun time, but if necessary, because that's where they got food poisoning.

Now the hard part—who to invite? Depending on how big your place is, you can't just put up fliers around town advertising your party (unless you live in a heavy metal concert in 1986). Plus, you don't want homeless families or drug dealers showing up. So, that leaves sending a text blast to a bunch of buds. Try to invite a variety of friends from all walks of life— doctors, policemen, and someone who works at a zoo. They can all learn from each other. If you're a hippie, a party is a quick way to let people know that you have a Pakistani friend at work. And if you're Pakistani, invite a hippie over for dinner, it will really cheer them up. Good luck and remember to not call the cops on yourself . . . even if you're out of control.

Lastly, have everyone bring a mix and take turns sharing music. Maybe turn it into a potluck so no one can claim to be sick from your delicious mayo salad. In general, in America (take note, fellow off-the-boat immigrants), it is good etiquette as a host to throw as much suspicion as you can on your guests.

> *"If the doors of perception were cleansed every thing would appear to man as it is, infinite. For man has closed himself up, till he sees all things through narrow chinks of his cavern."*
>
> —Eugene Mirman, 1983, repeating William Blake's quotation verbatim to scare his third grade teacher

Drinking and Drugs

Human beings, especially teenagers, artists, frat guys, depressed moms, ad execs from the '50s, Wolverine (technically *Homo superior*), and manipulative cult leaders, have always enjoyed imbibing mood- and mind-altering substances. Sometimes this is done to party, sometimes to understand the world, and sometimes to hide from the world you now understand.

Guess what? It is okay to drink and have fun, but it's not okay to become a spaced-out Drug Chump™—the kind so often mocked in '90s teen comedies and in the film *New Jack City*. Don't let drugs and booze control you, unless you're having a shitload of fun and don't mind spending the second half of your life regretting it. Some people have no problem dabbling in dope or drinking socially. Others need it like it's a drug, which it is, literally. Just the fact that drugs are so addictive that they can only be compared to themselves lets you know just what kind of Pandora's box we're talking about. The question is, how much is just right and how much is too much? Well, my friend Daniel once told me a story that I see as a perfect fable about drugs. . .

When Daniel was sixteen years old, he and a friend saw Steven Tyler, lead singer of America's quintessential sexy hard rock group Aerosmith, in a store near Kenmore Square in Boston. Everyone in Massachusetts, including myself (for reals), loves Aerosmith—again, because they are the masters of sexy old-school hard rock. ("It's all twos and fours, like fucking," Mr. Tyler has said about his music.)

Daniel and his friend, very nervously, approached Steven Tyler and told him how much they liked him and his music. Steven Tyler was very nice and thanked them very politely. They then left the store, thrilled to have met Boston's rock king. Seconds later, Steven Tyler ran out of the store, after them. They were like, "Hey, Steven Tyler, what's going on?" Steven Tyler then flexed his arm and mimed a heroin needle going into it and said, "Not cool."

So, the lesson is, it's okay to get fucked up once in a while, or even a little fucked up a lot, but it's not good to do so many drugs that you end up feeling compelled to run up to fans, warning them, through mime, to not repeat your past mistakes. Got it?

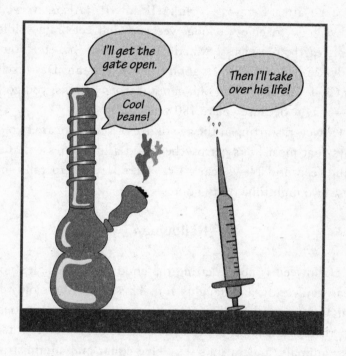

Also, a lot of people die from drug abuse, like Condoleezza Rice. Unlike Aerosmith, her drug wasn't drugs, but power, and she laced everything with it. I know she isn't dead *right* now, but I am hoping that this book becomes a classic, and when people read it a hundred years from now, they'll figure that Condoleezza Rice, whoever she was, died from smoking power.

Holidays (Non-Family)
Halloween, New Year's, and Maybe Another
....

There are basically three kinds of holidays: family, party, and serious-thing based. I'll talk about family holidays in another chapter—after I have a drink (JK alert!). Also, everybody knows how to enjoy a long weekend and celebrate soldiers, labor, earth, presidents, Martin Luther King Jr., etc. You already know how to have a good time on Veterans Day (excluding Civil War vets—you old, cantankerous drunks; you go too far—maybe because you're 180 years old?).

However, starting at the age of five or six, there are two holidays that most folks get psyched (and a little stressed) about: Halloween and New Year's Eve. Here, I want to talk about these two nighttime party holidays.

Halloween

Halloween is about letting the child in you out. It's about creativity, candy, and naughty fun. This is one of the only days that Congress allows businessmen to dress like celebrities or superheroes and ladies sixteen and older to dress as sexy witches, sexy animals, and various sexy blue-collar and administrative workers. (I doubt that an actual witch could get away with wearing a sexy witch outfit to her work, which is probably why some of the sexy witches you see on Halloween are ironically real witches exploring their sexuality.) The only other holiday that some people can cut loose on is Ash Wednesday. (By the way, Ash Wednesday is spooky if you don't know it's coming. They should consider reporting it on the evening news like they do Yom Kippur the night before.)

Anyway, back to Halloween. Don't eat apples with razors in them (especially electric). Be careful. Don't break people's cars or throw flaming bags of shit at anyone. And here are the costume ideas you asked for:

1. Stalin, Rasputin, or anyone from Russian history.
2. Characters made up in the style of Quentin Tarantino.
3. Batman and Jane. (Mix it up!)
4. A sex ed teacher who is the victim of identity theft. Think of a back story, motivation, etc. When people ask, "What are you?" Perform your rehearsed monologue to their delight!
5. An underwear repairman.
6. The inventor of the Bowflex as if he's stuck in the year 1826.
7. The Middle East.

Shut up and take this sub-prime loan!

8. A predatory lender disguised as Judge Judy.
9. Texas-sized _____ .
10. Rick Jenkins, founder of the Comedy Studio in Cambridge, Massachusetts.

New Year's Eve

New Year's Eve is exactly what it sounds like—it's a holiday of release and renewal. It's a chance to look back for a moment, and then go forward. The most important thing on New Year's is to make some resolutions. Try to think of a number of things you'd like to change or improve in your life and get to it around January 5. (You'll need a few days to recover.) Here are some suggested resolutions:

1. Stop referring to your husband/wife as "friend with benefits."
2. Stop the homeless.
3. If you make a child cry, donate money to a charity.
4. Try to do as many drugs as you can. (This one is only good if you have a real problem with accomplishing goals.)
5. Get married and stop being lonely.
6. Become the best at a board game of your choosing.
7. Run for a political office with the slogan, "The troops are the best."
8. Try to meet Hillary Clinton in an elevator (or on an escalator).
9. Start a band that gets a song on the Billboard Hot 100.
10. Befriend as many minorities as you can, including up to three Asians (unless you are one!) and two homosexuals (that's you!), depending on where you live. (Obviously not Iran or the Republican Party!!!!)

Oh! There's also Fourth of July. Just find a buddy and go to his house. Try not to blow up your hand. Before you do something involving fire and an explosive, ask yourself one question: "When people recall what I am about to do one year from today, is there a 25 percent chance (or higher) that people will start crying?" If the answer is yes, don't tie Roman candles to your arm and shoot them at people like a low-rent superhero (does sound fun though) or whatevs.

Staying Home
Murder Mystery, Movie Night, Crank Calls, Self-Touch, Hanging Out with Pals

• •

There's a lot of fun to be had at home. I think most of this stuff you know how to do, other than throwing a murder mystery party. To do that, just buy a kit, though. If you're having a few people over, invite people in groups of four, but no more than twelve.

Unlike a standardized test that simply figures out how good you are at memorizing information and regurgitating it (not like a bird), this quiz, designed at the University of Vermont by several grad students, will see how well you understand what you've just learned about the Night. . .

1. What are two rules of the Night Owners Code?
   a. *All of the above?*
   b. *If you abuse drugs, hide it from everyone you care about.*
   c. *Always carry a sword.*
   d. *I don't know.*
   e. *Underwear is neither inherently good nor bad on its own.* ▶

2. If you find yourself in danger in Chicago, where should you go?
    a. *The police.*
    b. *Wiener Circle.*
    c. *East Lansing, Michigan. (Hint: not correct answer.)*
    d. *Duck into a cool dive bar and tell everyone you used to play keyboards for Neutral Milk Hotel and that someone is after you.*

3. If you go to a party of someone under twenty-five with a date that is over twenty-five, what do you bring?
    a. *Seafood casserole.*
    b. *Pot brownies, horse tranc, and Ri-u-motherfuckin'-niti.*
    c. *Limbic. (This is the correct answer. Sorry. I couldn't risk you bringing horse tranc to a party, killing your friend, and having his conservative parents blame me on MSNBC)*
    d. *A cool mix CD and a crazy story about each song.*

4. Is it okay to go to the roof of tallest building in your town and jerk off into the street?
    a. *Yes.*
    b. *That is fucked up! What is wrong with you? But, I guess so.*
    c. *No! I'm telling my parents you wrote that! On second thought, I'm not going to tell them, because they are in their late '70s and they'd be mad and confused.*
    d. *If it's part of an internship and you get credit, sure.*

Family

From Raising a Family, to Surviving Being Raised by That Family. Just Now Added! The Holidays, Coming Out of the Closet, and More!

**"A family is like a rock 'n' roll band—
except you're born into it and they will
lend you money even if it's a bad idea."**

—Eugene Mirman, at a beach party in 1994,
describing what a family is to Morrissey

What Is Family?

When I taught the course *Family: What Is It?* at Princeton in 1981 (and later at Rutgers—but don't tell them), I would ask that question of all my students. The simple answer is that family is a loose genetic web of interconnected sex acts, a giant group of people who are tied together both legally and spiritually in a Fuck Web. Its antipuritan origin is the reason that no one publicly mentioned the concept of family before 1954. Its naughty roots are also why so many on the far right love saying the word now. (It is their emotional equivalent of secretly masturbating in a secluded area of Lord & Taylor.) No one will admit this, but it's true. No one would even deny it, fearing its mere mention as an admission of their guilt.

Family is also obviously much more: It is the backbone of life, a steadfast support system, but also a nasty neurosis-producer. Family is humanity's encoded genetic end-all goal. (Right? People who want children for healthy reasons, *and* people who want children to keep their marriage together.) Ultimately, family is the spirit rope of life, binding you to your family. Sometimes hanging on to that rope will save you, but other times that rope is part of a grand Tug-O-War Summer Camp Triathlon (mistakenly named, since the only game at this analogy-themed camp is tug-o-war). You can spend years tugging back and forth until you either fall into Life's Baggage-Laced Mud or pull your ailing, persnickety grandmother (and parents) and all their bullshit in.

Bonus Analogy Extension! Of course, if you're lucky, your whole family (except your dim, shitty uncle) all jump over the crisis-burdened mud into a magical rocket ship headed for the moon, where you all get ice cream, play Boggle, then return, and go to Harvard (because there's no Moon-Harvard yet—entrepreneur alert!!!). Afterwards, you begin your thriving career and start the whole process again, with a new tree branch that you make with your penis, vagina, or adoption papers.

Family is, after all, the beginning and the end, and doing it right is as important as doing it wrong, but for the opposite reasons. Like a genie (or a Eu-genie—I can't believe I made that joke and also that it took me this long to do it—this is what writers call a catch-22—no it isn't; stay alert), I will pretend that you have rubbed my tummy and asked me how to be a family, raise a family, and survive your family. P.S. I know you

2010 — A biblical misunderstanding leads to every-one in Colorado Springs giving up their first born.

2007—Beowulf is released in 3D, reminding people to not get tangled up with beautiful monsters, or you may father demonic, monster children.

2004 — George W. Bush signs "Families Are The Best" Act, reassuring families they are number one.

1999 — The AARP accepts a deal with the U.S. government over Medicaid, allowing some states to force the elderly back to work in mines.

1998 —Bill Clinton tries to lower the teen pregnancy rate by making oral sex "cool again." Though this does significantly lower teen pregnancy, it is also the catalyst for the "Barely Legal" Internet porn craze of the 2000s.

1991 — Congress passes a bill allowing parents to talk to their kids about marijuana use in a lighthearted way.

1985 — Spencer for Hire amends the meaning of "family" to include close friends and colleagues.

1975 — Stephen Spielberg's Jaws gives families a reason to sleep in the same giant bed again for the first time since 1905.

1969 — Jim Morrison is arrested for exposing himself at a concert in Miami, worrying parents that their kids are into "crazy shit." Most parents forbid children from going outside, especially to Vietnam.

1972 — All in the Family redefines sitcoms and family perceptions.

1961 — The film adaptation of A Raisin in the Sun is released.

1960 —Because of his naïveté and lack of formal education, Nikita Khrushchev embarrassingly introduces his concept of "The Authority Shoe" as Communism's answer to unruly children. Dr. Spock issues harsh rebuke.

1959 — Sammy Davis, Jr., and Loray White get divorce. First time marriage problems are discussed in American media.(Compared to the French, who openly discussed such things since the late 1700s as a result of Marie Antoinette's excesses).

1958 — Sammy Davis, Jr. marries Loray White.

1957 — Elvis releases, "(Let Me Be Your) Teddy Bear" and inspires a generation of horny teens to start families out of wedlock, Korean War vets issue statement saying, "That's not what we fought for."

1954 — Scott Bakula is born to parents Sally and J. Stewart Bakula. This is considered the first "modern" family. Before that, families consisted mostly of confused and disorganized immigrants.

1946 — Benjamin McLane Spock (i.e. Dr. Spock) publishes The Common Sense Book of Baby and Child Care.

TIMELINE OF FAMILY

don't rub a genie's tummy to make a wish, but you are the one who did it, not me. Sorry, I'm defensive. I take back the things I said that you would like me to take back.

The Number One Rule of Family: No Molestation, Please

The first thing in any family is to not sexually assault the other members. Though this sounds obvious, the statistics from *Law and Order: Special Victims Unit* prove otherwise. This rule is doubly true for uncles, according to several songs by the Who. Also, I recommend not sex-attacking the friends of any members of your family. Do you really want your son's schoolmate to be like, "I don't want to go to your birthday sleepover, because your mom always tries to oralize me while I'm sleeping—and she isn't hot like Andie MacDowell."

About 35 percent of all family-based squabbles come from sexual misconduct (based on a statistic I bet I could find somewhere—or if you like, I'll pretend I read it in the Bible). Pop culture has countless examples: the ancient play *Oedipus Rex*, Aerosmith's "Janie's Got a Gun" (and "Uncle Salty" about two decades prior), and even the music of Sigmund Freud.

If all that isn't enough to convince you, you should watch 1994's *Spanking the Monkey* as a clear example of the difficulties involved.

Spousing It Up: Being a Good Husband or Wife
(Or Both, You Lucky Bisexual Recipient of Hermaphroditic Party-Time)

Think of a marriage as some sort of structure of leaning sticks that need each other to stand. I bet there's a name for that kind of structure. In life, that structure is called a marriage: a lifelong bond between two people (generally a man and a man—this book takes place in Bill O'Reilly's nightmare). You're each other's yin and yang, creating balance, if that's what yin and yang do. I bet it is. What makes a marriage work? Three possible things: (1) deep love, (2) an overwhelming sense of obligation, (3) a massive power imbalance. You can also have shades of all three. The first type of marriage requires work, but is great.333333333xzzzzzzzzzz zzzzzzzzzfrrrrrrrrrrrrrrrrrrep---". Sorry, my cat stepped on the keyboard and I decided to leave it. Anyway . . .

One important thing is to give each other space. Have some interests of your own, so you don't suffocate each other. Also, periodically check in by asking, "What's wrong?" If your spouse says, "Nothing," in an angry or sulking tone, slap them, and go, "I asked you a question, you wuss! Now, what's wrong?????!!!!!" This will help open the channels of communication. And try to smile a little. "Good feelings are contagious," I always say. But then I add, "So is the clap, so don't betray each other's trust."

Bro'in' Down: Being a Bro to Yo Bro and a Sistah to Yo Sistah

(Hahahahhahahahahahha! I'll give five dollars to whoever first figures out what culture's slang I just appropriated. And before you get mad at me, just consider how racist *Rush Hour 3* is and 4 will be. We're all complicit in its popularity and cultural cannibalism, except me, who didn't see it and hates it. However, on a side note—you should never touch a black man's radio—unless that black man is your friend and not a crazy caricature.)

Being siblings can be a wonderful, rewarding relationship. Most siblings filter for each other the outside world (and their parents). They can protect each other, help each other, and even be a little competitive—which in modern times can be good (Oasis is living proof of the triumphs of sibling rivalry), but in ancient times it generally led to assassinations. Plus, siblings are a great way to find out about Guns 'N' Roses. (I guess that's a very specific example, but it's also true.)

Much of being a good sibling is clear, but just in case you're a selfish asshole, I'll list the basic golden guidelines (referred to as The Main 5 in books on adolescents) to being the sibling you wish your siblings were to you:

1. Share.
2. Give them space. (Let them make out in peace, and in exchange they'll let you tag along to the mall sometimes.)
3. Train them for battle with swords, small arms, and hand-to-hand combat.
4. If it's a sister, beat up anyone she tries to date.
5. If it's a brother, hire a prostitute for him when he turns sixteen (even if you're eleven) so that he becomes a man.

That's it. If you follow those rules, everything should work out. One criticism that I hear a lot from myself about the last thing I wrote is that it doesn't challenge conventional gender roles, and in fact reinforces them. That's true. But maybe that's my way of empowering you to change them. Or maybe not? I will never reveal my true intent, because like the C?A, I gain my power from secrecy.

Parenting: Children and Kids
They Are the Same Thing (at First!)
....

For the last decade I've rented out the Times Square Marriott and held a forty-eight-hour crash course in child rearing—instead of carrying eggs like in junior high, I make attendees carry cantaloupe and I prepare new fathers to function with a blood alcohol level of 0.27 percent (which for most would induce blackout, severely impair motor function, and put them on the verge of involuntary restroom use in a non-restroom setting). Some notable alums include: Martin Short, J. K. Rowling, and Paul Thomas Anderson.

Being a parent is as easy as counting to one million—most anyone can do it, but it's exhausting—and periodically rewarding (like when you reach five hundred thousand)—and once you're done, you are not sure why you did it—but it was worth it.

As a first time parent, you have to know when to hold them, know when to fold them, and know one other thing, I think. That's right, raising a child is a lot like playing poker in the Old West. As you may have suspected, I don't mean fold literally (though you do *have* to know when to fold a child, which is, of course—never). By "fold" I mean "abuse." Do not abuse your child. You're probably like, "But I already don't hit them! You're as bad and meddlesome as Big Government!" Stop being so defensive. There are many kinds of abuse. A lot of abuse comes from being unsupportive, negative, or overdemanding.

(I'm talking to you, parents of Asian, Indian, and Eastern European immigrants!)

If your child is a fuckup, it's okay to come down hard on them (deny them access to Facebook, limit their exposure to holo-porn, or do a Memory Wipe—the last two are to keep this book relevant until the year 2085), but try not to have the kinds of expectations that they rebel too much against. Every Almost-Grown-Up (teenager) gets mad and participates in unsound behavior—which can be anything from drinking beer to stealing beer with a gun (or crossbow). Sometimes Almost-Grown-Ups act out to explore the world, and sometimes it's to hurt you. So, try to set hard but positive expectations, but not the kind that make someone turn into a violent, unstable nutball. (I'm talking to you Mike Huckabee—whoever he was.)

To help you tell the difference between what is abuse and what is a good punishment, I've written out some ideas for you. Feel free to improvise and use these as a guideline, but don't stray so far that you are reported to child services—by your own conscience!

Abuses to Avoid

1. Withholding love. Never link your love to your child's accomplishments (unless they are truly, truly incompetent).

2. Waterboarding. This is not an acceptable punishment for children—especially ones who have absolutely no provable links to terrorist organizations. (However, if you suspect your child may be an al-Qaeda operative, please call the White House right away at 202-456-1111.)

3. Never put a child in a "Punishment Bag."

4. Sexual humiliation—don't make them strip and do embarrassing things and then take pictures of it. It's not the deterrent you're looking for. There's an old Norwegian saying, "A boy that's been sexually humiliated grows up to be a man who also has." Now you know why you never hear Norwegian sayings—they're accurate, but too specific.

5. Never tell your kid that the crisis in the Middle East is their fault— even as a gag. In general, don't make them feel responsible for global conflicts.

Never put a child in a Punishment Bag.

Healthy Punishments for Children

1. Deny certain luxuries like television, sleepovers, and vodka tonics (if they're sixteen or older). Never send them to sleep without dinner or deny them access to a bathroom.

2. Explain tax fraud in detail. Do it each time they disobey you.

3. Make them spend a week like it's 1826—without electricity, having to use an outhouse, with outdated medical care, constructing America's first railroads, etc. Not too dangerous, but super effective. The Norwegians also say, "A child who reads by candlelight for a week is easy to control."

4. Make them dig a ditch. Don't tell them it's their grave, but hint at it.

5. Instead of a fun birthday present, give them something depressing, like a photograph of injured soldiers from the Civil War.

Make them dig a ditch. Don't tell them it's their grave, but hint at it.

Instead of a fun birthday present, give them something depressing, like a photograph of injured soldiers from the Civil War.

Babies
· · · · · · · · · ·

What is a baby? Well, a baby is nothing more than a tiny person who makes no sense. What does this mean? Mostly, it is important to set your expectations low. Most problems arise when parents want their babies to react to verbal commands. The two important things to remember about babies are to feed them and to have them puke on your back a little. Everything else will work itself out.

If you can think of a way to develop a diaper that sends a baby's poo into another realm, do it. An interdimensional diaper is probably the invention most sought-after by new fathers. This assumption is mostly based on my recollection of the trailer for *Three Men and a Baby*.

How to Make a Baby Cry More
(Unnecessary, but Fun)

Sometimes, as a parent, you need to unwind. And one of the best ways to unwind is to briefly unshackle yourself from the chains of conventional parenthood and taunt your baby a bit. A few quick, harmless ways to cut loose:

1. Using your hands as puppets, act out an episode of *The Wire* (from the middle of a season, so they get confused).
2. Wash them using chowder.
3. Put fireproof gel on your arm and light it on fire. Then scream and scream!

Adopting a Foreign Baby

Foreign babies can be a great source of baby. However, some will try to sneak you an injured baby with a tail. Be careful. The number one thing most parents forget to do is get their potential baby fingerprinted to be sure it does not have a criminal record. If it comes up clean, adopt it. Make sure you tell it you love it all the time (in its native tongue). Adopted babies (especially foreign) need special attention because they are victimized in so many fairytales.

Ten Rules for Raising a Child

There are ten guiding principles that, if never betrayed, will result in a child as happy and well adjusted as you first believe your child is when he says something you think is brilliant, but is just sort of smart for a two-year-old.

1. Disappointment is more powerful than anger.
2. Tell them you love them, even if you don't mean it.
3. No playing with fire until s/he is eleven years old. (It's okay to let them use it for heat or to forge weapons.)
4. If you tell a child s/he is ugly, make sure to have proof.
5. Survival skills—a six-year-old who can survive in the woods for a week is ready for school—and life. As the child gets older it becomes less impressive, so try to make them do it before they are nine. However, *never* leave a toddler in a forest.
6. ABC—Always Be Cee-ing (what they are up to).
7. Forgive (not just them, but also me for rule six).
8. Seriously, *never* leave a toddler in a forest.
9. Make audiocassettes of people fucking and play them at night once they turn seventeen (fourteen, for ladies in South Carolina, as of this writing!!!!!!) *Yeah!*
10. Let them know they can talk to you about anything and that you will pretend you're "cool with it" at first.

Teenagers: Oh, Boy
....

Once your tween becomes a teen, it's time to put on your "Oh, Shit" gloves and get ready to parent. Other than myself, most teenagers are trouble. Their bodies are telling them to try drugs and touch their genitals to as much stuff as possible. Some parents scare children with tales of a frightful afterlife where they'll be punished forever for misbehaving, while others warn about the difficulty of raising a baby at the age of fifteen.

To help a teenager (or "young adult," as faggy liberal parents would have you believe—sorry, some dude from Swampscott, Massachusetts, wrote the last part in 1986 and I was unable to stop him) become a Grown-Up, you're going to need a few things: "Oh, Shit" gloves, a very stern facial expression, and a command of pseudopsychological mumbo-jumbo, and gin.

Like whatever that thing is in the first Indiana Jones movie where he swaps out the sand for the valuable thing-a-doodle, you have to trick your teenager into thinking they are experimenting, while in fact everything is safe. Try to not have everything collapse on your head and then get ruined by an evil German guy with native warriors.

> *"Sometimes a very specific analogy is more trouble than it's worth. Unless we change our monetary system—not to a gold standard, but to a trouble standard—then this type of analogy would be a great way to make a living."*
>
> —Eugene Mirman, speaking at a poorly attended conference titled Teenagers and Inflation

What I'm really suggesting is that at the age of fourteen you make your child a terrible martini. That's why you need gin. Not for you (though partake if you like), but for them. One sip of that juniper-berry ether (especially if you overdo the vermouth) and they will not try it for at least another four years. Show me one child that has a dry martini at the age of fourteen and grows up to have a drinking problem. (This is an example of a "misargument," which, though false from inception, is nonetheless unbeatable. Use them as often as possible.)

> *"Also, I forgot to add that the expression 'There's no such thing as a free lunch' would no longer apply as much."*
>
> —Eugene Mirman, speaking later at the same conference

In-Laws

In-laws get a bad rap, but they aren't so bad—some are more pleasant than your own family (especially if your father was an alcoholic—right, children of Edgar Allan Poe, Joseph McCarthy, and Mel Gibson?). In some cultures, it can take almost a decade before your in-laws are comfortable enough to order you around. That means you have ten years to stop them from controlling you before it's too late, which is far longer than most protagonists get in movies to save the world. (Most have to do it within an hour and a half.)

Surviving the Holidays

Most families love each other a lot, would die for each other, laugh and laugh and laugh together, but also can only handle being around each other for about sixteen hours (one dinner, one breakfast, and mostly sleep). Regardless of age, grandparents treat parents like children, children treat parents like bad cops, and personalities can clash—especially if you're all like each other and refuse to admit it. According to *Ladies' Home Journal*, people only want to be reminded they are fat, have the wrong job, or are gay and a disappointment twice before they're ready to leave.

Like a soldier or spy who has certain mental and physical defenses against being attacked, so must you. About two weeks before a major family-related holiday, you need to start preparing yourself for "fun battle."

Aggravating people can be found anywhere. Every once in a while, you go into a shop, have a meeting with someone, or go on a date with a person who's really annoying or aggressively stupid. That person who rubbed you the wrong way is someone's brother/aunt/daughter/father. There is a family, maybe full of people like that, who all get together a few times a year and fight. If it's your family, ready yourself. Two simple exercises are (1) pretend you're adopted, and (2) respond to everything anyone says with, "That's nice."

Good Uncle, Bad Influence

"Being an uncle is like being a rock star no one but your niece or nephew has heard of."

—Eugene Mirman, from his shitty novel *An Uncle's Tale.*

World's Number One Grandparents

Your job is simple: Provide candy, stories, and twenty dollars in every greeting card. That's it.

"Grandparents are to grandkids what great-grandparents are to parents—grandparents."

—Eugene Mirman, from his award-winning docudrama *Roundabout Quoties*

Wait! I almost forgot: To the best of your ability, try to treat your own kids like grown-ups, letting them make decisions, have sex, and live their lives mostly the way they'd like to (interfering only when it's maddening, but funny). You'll have

an easier time seeing your grandkids if you don't create insur-
mountable resentment against you and your overbearing opinions. I know, your kids should appreciate you more. I agree.
You fed them, washed their poop-covered poop-holders, put
them through college, and cried them to sleep (hopefully not).
And here's the thing—you're probably even right. But here's the
other thing—it's sometimes more important to be quiet than
right. Okay? Great. Because this is about spending time with
your family, so stop correcting everyone all the time, you old,
overcontrolling jerk. *Note to grown-up parents:* Try to be nice
to your overbearing parents and pretend to do what they say.
Thanks!

Dealing with Parents (as a Kid)
....

Your parents want the best for you (probably). So, everything
they do is to that end. Sometimes they don't understand that
just because you listen to heavy metal doesn't mean you're a
misogynistic Satan worshipper (but it could, depending on
how easily influenced you are). So the best way to get what you
want is to see things from their point of view then anticipate it,
and accomplish it. Once you do that, you'll be in charge. Also,
don't forget to not betray their trust. Just kidding. Of course
you will betray their trust—but do it less when you may get
caught. Winning back your parents' trust is super annoying,
so try not to be too deceitful, unless of course you are gay and
they are homophobic, or they are crazy, prudish control freaks,
then treat them like North Korea (talking about the threat but
ultimately ignoring it to the detriment of the United States and
the world).

Disappointing Your Parents (and Me) by Getting on a Reality TV Show

....

I have to say I cannot decide what is less respectable, having a pile of anonymous dicks shooting jizz on you (drives parents *crazy*) or being on reality television (public and often *more* humiliating, depending on the number of anonymous dicks; probably more humiliating than the jizz of nine dicks or less). My guess is, reality television is the higher virtue, but I'm (1) probably wrong, and (2) easily swayed by my own puritanical second-guessing (unless it's an old-timey talent contest, like *American Idol* or *Project Runway*—those are okay, I guess).

If you're a petty person (or can pretend) and hate your parents, I'll help you exact this poor but hurtful revenge. Plus, you'll also receive a lifetime of going from crappy nightclub opening to crappy nightclub opening for cash. This is what you should do:

For girls: Videotape yourself beating the shit out of your "boyfriend" in a hotel room for one of three reasons—either he (1) tattooed "What up?" on his dick, (2) cheated on you with Paula Abdul, or (3) was disrespectful to his mother.

For guys: Videotape yourself beating yourself up (i.e., a literal version of the old "why are you hitting yourself?" routine) for one of the same reasons.

Once you have made your video, mail it to:

I'm an Asshole Who Hates My Parents
c/o NBC
30 Rockefeller Plaza
New York City, NY 10112

If you are more interested in having premarital sex with other teenagers along with being humiliated, send the tape to:

I'm a Horny Asshole Who Hates My Parents
c/o MTV
1515 Broadway
New York, NY 10036

It's that simple. Just fill out some paperwork and send it in. Depending on the show, when your parents see you eat bugs for money or whatever, they'll know they were dicks to you and should have respected you more. Basically, reality television is a great replacement for attempted suicide to "show them."

Dealing with Parents (as an Adult)

Your parents will always see you as their child. It's because you are. As a result, they'll always tell you what to do. Still, there is something you can do to get your parents to stop forwarding you joke e-mails that are either politically misguided or unfunny in a slightly misogynistic or racist way. Here it is:

Tell them you are pregnant. This will distract them. (If you are male, tell them anyway. Parents love to focus their energies on scientific miracles.)

Interracial/Interfaith/Inter-????? Marriage
••

Hopefully, by the time you are reading this, most racial tension in America and abroad (except in Russia) will have dissipated. So this whole section will be moot. In case it isn't, I guess probably the best thing to do is believe in yourself.

There isn't a lot you can do about how strangers on the street treat you (other than race-changing cream and disguises), but there is quite a bit you can do to train your family or loved ones to stop being unpleasant and bigoted.

A simple way to get your spouse's family to behave decently is to be disarmingly self-deprecating about your race, religion, or ethnicity. Once they get comfortable around you and join in with their own stereotypes, act upset (which you might also be in real life!). This will make them very, very uncomfortable. Now you have all the power! (This only works on people who don't want to think of themselves as prejudiced.)

In an extreme case—e.g., if you are a disenfranchised Muslim woman and a Hassidic Jew who've both shunned their demanding, restrictive religions—you're facing an overwhelming battle. Most likely, your families will never accept your marriage. Though on the one hand this is very troubling, on the other, you can relieve your own stress by constantly taunting them.

Lastly, what to do with the classic black guy marrying a white woman scenario? No one before me has had the courage to reveal this secret, but it is customary in a white (especially Catholic) family for the fiancé to beat the shit out of the father. After that, everybody gets along. I know, I'm revealing an ancient secret. But that is how so many interracial marriages first began—with a whopping.

Figuratively Coming Out of the Closet
Literally Revealing You Are Gay
....

Telling your family, especially your parents, that you're gay is the hardest thing a person who is not in physical danger has to do (if his family is homophobic—if your whole family is gay, then telling them you are color-blind is the most difficult thing).

> *"Try telling someone you're gay sometime. It's a good exercise."*
> —Eugene Mirman, opening Oliver North to new perspectives at a fundraiser for the Wildlife Conservation Fund in 2007

Hopefully, soon no one will care that people are gay. It's exhausting and depressing that people worry about strangers being gay and constantly imagine gay sex in anger. But people do, because they fear what they don't understand and some probably just think it's gross (but that doesn't make it wrong—the way that Korean blood soup—haejangguk or seonjiguk—may be gross to some, but to Koreans, it's just good ol' blood soup, great for a hangover and great to fight anemia—just like homosexuality).

The best place to tell your parents you are a homosexual person from now on (no changing your mind back after college, okay?) is at a fancy restaurant. (If you want to come out to a friend and tell them you're in love with them, the best place to do that is late, late at night at someone's house when you're both drunk.)

Pick a nice place, one where it would be embarrassing for someone (e.g., WASP-y parents) to act up. In the middle of the meal, show them a *Vogue* magazine (if you're a guy) or a *Popular Mechanics* (if you're a lady) and go, "This is me now, and you have to accept it." If they are confused, whisper, "I'm gay." The point of this roundabout exercise is the joy of deduction. Giving your parents clues and making them figure out that you're gay will give them a sense of accomplishment that will balance their initial shock. Instead of going, "My son is gay?!" they will go, "Son, thank you for this riddle, and we have solved it . . . you are gay!" Do you see how in the first scenario they are shocked, but in the second, they are proud problem solvers? That's how you come out. Feel free to give them more clues to draw the process out longer. Perhaps a box of Lucky Charms? Maybe wear a full length fur coat and make yourself shiny with hot oils? It's up to you.

Three things may happen:

1. Kind, accepting parents may find it difficult, but will love you for who you are.
2. Some parents will ignore it and never react to the information again, but treat you like they did before, only slightly weirder.
3. Prejudiced, somewhat assholey parents won't accept it, will disown you, but secretly always regret it (especially the mom).

Although my scenario creates the best odds for it working out well, you have to be prepared for all three possibilities. If it's the last, the important thing is to leave the meal having zinged them. Here are three witty things that you can say on your way out:

1. "The years 1954–1988 called, they want their world view back."

2. "Hey, I was trying to tell you I was gay. I didn't realize that you were coming out of the closet to me—as assholes! See ya!"

3. "I'll be on Cape Cod, in San Francisco, or in Northampton, Massachusetts—call me if you want to party. I mean, if you want to be a family again. I already miss you."

The years 1954–1988 called; they want their world view back.

Hello. Am I speaking to the parents of a kid who just came out of the closet?

You did it. You are the proud owner of huge balls. Now call a supportive friend, go get a drink, and have a good laugh or cry. Don't forget to love yourself!

The Heart, the Penis, and Mrs. Vagina

Love, Sex, and How to Find a Mate Before You Die—to Do It with, Marry, or Bothsies!!!

> **"I need two quotes here. One from a great two-thousand-year-old play, that lets you know that I have a deep but witty understanding of love, and one from a modern, mischievous rapper. That way, twenty- and thirty-something Vassar grads who read *Elle* magazine will know that this girl really *gets it!*"**
>
> —Eugene Mirman, right now to you

Love
......

One of the biggest questions in people's lives is how to find a mate (or mates—if you're pagan, lead an alternative lifestyle, or are a member of Led Zeppelin). From the age of four you are taught that life's mission is to find a husband/wife/life-partner and to fall in love. Whether it's through music or John Cusack movies, everyone knows that love is the most important thing.

But things can get pretty complicated on the Driveway of Love. (Oops! A *driveway* is where you park, and a *parkway* is where you drive! I forgot. Sorry.)

I first fell in love in second grade. There was a game everyone played where you'd run around on the playground and try to kiss each other. I forget what it was called, but something like Catch and Kiss or Unaware Child-On-Child Sex Attack. I know it wasn't called Electronic Stratego, because there was a totally different game named that.

Because I was foreign and weird, I was never included in Catch and Kiss. Still, one day I decided that I would Catch and Kiss a beautiful girl I had a crush on. However, instead of doing it at recess, I decided to do it when school let out. So as the bell rang, signaling everyone to go home, I (like a fucking Ninja!) kissed Kristen (fake name—haha) on the cheek and ran home. That helped solidify to the other kids that they were right, I was a loose cannon—a dangerous lunatic who did not understand how things worked in America.

Still, for that one second, Kristen and I were in love. We never spoke before or after. I think she may even be a bit of a fatty now (probably not). It doesn't matter. The point is, you should take what you want—it's the only way. Unless someone seems upset; then don't. Okay, great. Let's do this!

> "Life is a freeway and not a highway. Love is a sedan, not a rose. In conclusion, love is something different from what you think, but very practical."
>
> —Eugene Mirman, to a group of high teenagers waiting to buy tickets to the last Phish concert at Coney Island

What Is Love?
·····················

Love is both simple and complicated. Countless wars have been fought over it—e.g., Vietnam, the Spanish-American War, and World War I. The First Anglo-Chinese war—also known as the First Opium War—was actually fought over an incredibly awkward date. Half of mankind spends its time trying to make sure there is food, while the other half is trying to figure out love and relationships. (That is a real fact from a Stanford study.) Way more than 240 plays have been written about love, and there are close to 4,000 paintings warning young adults about love's dangers. All sorts of people sing about it—young, old, happy, strong, Mexican, Australian (probably), and girls. There's even a common belief in many countries (mostly Japan and Nigeria) that cats write love poems to each other. Silly foreigners—no, they don't.

THE HISTORY OF LOVE

Adam and Eve.

Abraham and Sara.

47 B.C.E. Caesar and Cleopatra.

1380s–1390s "Canterbury Tales" are written. Nobody was impressed.

1776 American Revolution, Declaration of Independence.

1895 Amusement parks make dating a reality for the American middle class.

1915 Jazz becomes popular.

1923 Teenagers start eating jazz, renting motel rooms with hot tubs and having reefer orgies. The first reefer baby is born Harry Smith (known for the Anthology of American Folk Music).

December 12, 1957 Jerry Lee Lewis and Myra Gale Brown get married.

1958 Jerry Lee Lewis British tour is cancelled from scandal that Myra is Lewis' thirteen-year-old cousin; world discovers that love is difficult.

1960 Birth control pill is introduced in United States, people start to really party. Working folks switch from anal to vaginal intercourse.

1968 Jim Morrison of The Doors is very sexy.

1985 Growing Pains airs, though most sexual content is removed at star Kirk Cameron's request, nobody seems to mind a supporting character named Boner.

1992 Woody Allen and Soon-Yi Previn openly have relationship, Allen declares, "the heart wants what the heart wants."

1996 E-mail becomes a popular way to apologize for bad dates and tell people you want to just be friends.

1998 Blast from the Past—a charming, underrated romantic comedy starring Alicia Silverstone and Brendan Fraser with Christopher Walken, Sissy Spacek and Dave Foley is released. National Divorce rate drops 5%!

2005 Reality TV helps people connect in a way that was impossible 2000 years ago.

2006 Slobodan Miloševic dies and leaves behind a book of bawdy love poems which won't be published for another twenty years.

2007 Daylight savings changes allowing for an extra hour of love making in middle-class households.

2010 A new type of music called "Unprotected-Sex-Core" terrifies parents.

2012 Because of "Unprotected-Sex-Core," every morning high school students make love in cafeterias under tarps. Teen pregnancy goes up 2400% (making every girl pregnant and 18% of boys).

2026 Slobodan Milošević's book of poems is published to scathing reviews and poor sales. Oh well. Whoever suggested not publishing it in the first place was right.

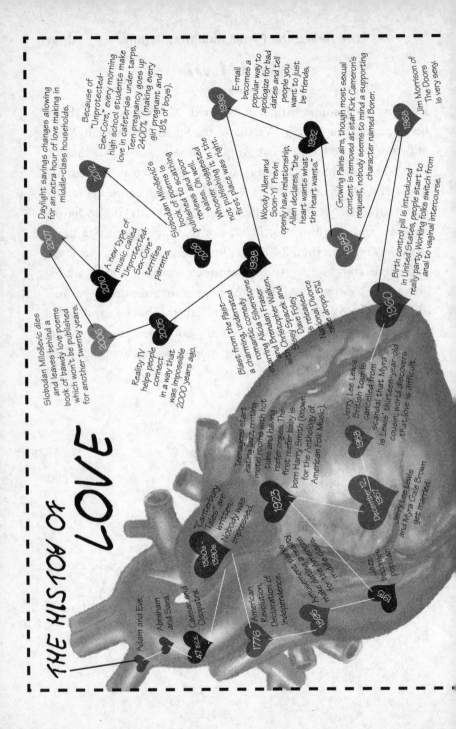

The History of Love

·······················

The Six Signs You're in Love

1. You can't wait to see them/you think about them all the time
2. When you're with them, you forget to go to pee for thirty-two days straight.
3. When you watch people fight on reality TV, it makes you cry because they will never be happy, like you are, because you are in love.
4. You try to look really nice for them, even if you've been dating for three years. (This is sadly also true for last-ditch efforts of making a failed relationship work.)
5. You ask someone to marry you and couldn't care less about all the ass (or balls! Right, ladies?) you didn't get/can't have.
6. You really relate to *The Princess Bride* because of how similar that story is to your own life.

How Do I Get Someone to Fall in Love with Me?

··

On April 5, 1998, I was awoken by a phone call at 2:30 a.m. It was Gérard Depardieu—he fell hard for a femme fatale and needed advice. It's a pretty common occurrence to be in love with someone, but have it feel like they don't know you exist, right? That feeling is the plot of several movies, so it must be a universal feeling; otherwise, Hollywood fucked up. But they didn't, because they love money. So it is common.

There are two kinds of love: Real Love and Quick Love. Both can happen quickly, but one is based on a real knowledge of a person and the other is based on characteristics you've given them that may be wrong. Both result in sexual experimentation, so it's okay. Here's how you get someone to fall for you.

Quick Love

This is sometimes mistaken for lust. It is not lust. People genuinely misunderstand each other and trick themselves into believing they are in love. At the worst, they go out for four months and end it with an unwanted pregnancy. At best, they have a passionate love affair for two weeks and then return to whatever country each is from.

All this involves is pointing at the person you "love" and capturing them with an imaginary lasso. Once they hop over to you, whisper something in a made up language (for instance: "Ke foo pé lableu?" or "Wapoo toot feyfai?") and then ask them to show you around the city.

Real Love

You must find out everything about them by hiring a detective. Then get them to go to a café with you using whatever means are necessary. (This may involve framing them for a small crime and then offering them a way out—it works, trust me.) Obviously, if you can get them to come to the café without using deceit, it will be easier and you'll have less stuff to keep track of. Do not take them to dinner. It will be uncomfortable and you will find out too much irrelevant stuff about their family and first job.

When you are at the café, tell them that you've had them followed and that you'd like to have sex. Congratulations—you are in love! Unlike television, in real life, people are impressed with what's sometimes called "stalking." Once they find out how hard you tried, they totally go for it!

Quick note: A great way to "accidentally" fall in love is to set up what I call a Stanley Milgram Date. Basically, you fake a psychological study that is somewhat traumatic to your object of desire. Then, when they are mentally and emotionally shattered, offer them some soup and some comfort. After it's over, invite them to a café. Nice job—you just fell in love—and it was no accident.

Special Author's Self-Congrats
I really provide Life Tools! Congrats to me!

Dating and Relationships
· ·

Dating is not easy. Ask most people between the ages of sixteen and twenty-two and they'll tell you they've never been on a "date," that they just hook up with friends and acquaintances. (This fact is not based on information. But it's still true.) Ask anyone born after 9/11 and they'll tell you the idea of dating is scary and probably gross. (This will no longer be true in 2025.)

Still, some form of dating can be found in even the most backward cultures, like Maine and Kuwait. Everyone from celebrities to the president has been on a date. Teddy Roosevelt went on more than a hundred dates before he married his childhood playmate, Edith Kermit Carow.

Whoever is in the band Def Leppard goes on dates still, even though their musical peak was more than fifteen years ago. That is how popular dating is.

What Should We Do Tonight?

Everybody is always looking for a great idea for a date (or a "pre-hook-up activity"). If you can do something romantic, special, or fun, it's the difference between starting a relationship, or going home alone and broken, unsure of where you went wrong. (If you're a guy, you went wrong by talking about yourself way, way, way too much, and if you're a girl, sadly, it was something superficial like a horn or antlers—guys hate girls with defensive bone-like protrusions. Shallow, but true.)

The best way to remove some of the pressure from the awkward intimacy of a date (for both of you, or all three, if you're lucky—*insert cat-like noise*) is to do an activity that's both interesting and a distraction of sorts. After close to a decade of going on dates for various research institutes and pharmaceutical companies, I have compiled several ideas for some unique dates:

"A simple way to keep someone interested is to be erratic and emotionally unavailable, but another way is to wear a mask and use different voices."

—Eugene Mirman, 1995, addressing the UN,
to their surprise and dismay

Super Fun Dates

1. Build a fort and camp out in it.
2. Rob a bank.
3. Go to a museum dressed as Nancy Reagan (both of you).

Superfun date: Go to a museum dressed as Nancy Reagan (both of you).

4. Have a duel using guns with rubber bullets.
5. Have dinner on a raft you built in the ocean. Don't forget a flare gun! If you think make-up sex is fun, wait till you have rescued-by-the-coast-guard sex.

How to Keep Things Interesting

The number one thing is to remain the sexy person you were when you first met. Before going to bed, you should both put on tattered loincloths and wrestle. That's the spirit! Maybe bring some chocolate-dipped strawberries to bed . . . (*cat noise*—again). If you're embarrassed to bring desserts into the bedroom, that's normal, don't worry. You don't have to. Instead, consider something savory like pad Thai or corn chowder. Even though dieticians don't recommend eating right before bed, most Fucketicians do. (I am both sorry and not sorry that I wrote Fucketician.)

He Wants to Blah Blah and She Wants to Whah Blah Whah: Compromising in a Relationship

I am constantly getting text messages from religious leaders seeking my advice in their relationships. They always ask basically the same thing, "I am an important, forty-six-year-old rabbi and my wife is a twenty-eight-year-old professional wrestler. When I get home I want to watch *Star Trek: Voyager*, but she wants me to clean the basement so she can turn it into some kind of '70s rec room (she claims). Really, she wants to distract me so she can watch *CSI: Miami* (which she Tivos—so it's not time-sensitive). I'm fine with watching *CSI*. I just want to watch *Voyager* first."

That rabbi has a classic I want/she wants scenario. It's the theme of every relationship and movie (even *Serpico*, I bet).

Some psychologists suggest drawing straws and the one with the longer straw gets to decide what to watch first. Other psychologists suggest that the person with the shorter straw should decide. I would pay up to four hundred dollars to watch those two groups draw straws to decide who was right.

To me, both fake scenarios seem to miss the point. Well, good luck. Talk it out and try to be reasonable. Maybe take turns? Do the thing where you each have a knife in one hand, tie the other to your spouse's hand, and do battle? It's a good way to decide something and a wonderful twist on foreplay. Too much of a chicken? All right. How about a game of Rummikub every Monday evening, winner gets to make all team decisions for the week? If it's really bad, you can always get divorced. First, though, try to be a good listener and don't forget to open your Heart-Ears. Seriously, don't be a jerk and take turns doing what you each want (unless what you want hurts either of your bottoms).

A fun exercise that can help improve a relationship is to watch ten minutes of a romantic comedy before you start your day. Let Meg Ryan into your heart, and she in turn will help you hide from the pain. Contrary to what you may have heard, hiding from the pain is the number one way to avoid difficult situations. Solving the problem can often take years and might not even work. Did you know that some ostriches (who are famous—but with a different kind of fame from Kurt Russell—for burying their head in the sand) live for two hundred years? At least they think they do. Most don't even understand years. Okay. I don't want to overwhelm you with too much knowledge. After all, the human brain is about four liters big (or less) and if too much knowledge about one topic enters it in one moment, it will command the body to shut down or binge-eat, and I don't want to make you do that. So let's take a deep breath, have another sip of wine, and move on.

Moving in Together: Uh-Oh, or Yay!!!!!

This can be a wonderful thing, the beginning of a new beginning, or it can be rough, like riding a bull on the edge of the sun! One of the hardest years of marriage is the first. Now that culture has figured out a way to get around marriage, by just moving in together, you still have some of the stresses, but life has given you a chance to take marriage for a test drive. Enjoy the ride; this may be the car for you.

Just remember to take a step back sometimes and ask

yourself one question, "Am I happy?" If the answer is, "Yes," be careful. When people hastily say yes, sometimes it's because they're afraid of thinking "No." However, if the answer is "Not really, but sort of," then you're on the right track. Things are better than you think.

Breaking Up and the Fallout . . .

Breaking up can be very hard to do. It can also be easy. If it's easy for you, you are most likely a whimsical, sexy sociopath or simply fickle. If this is the case, you will have no problem spending much of your life in the endless tumult of dating, until you are old and either permanently alone, or fortunate enough to briefly marry a young stripper who really, really loves you.

However, if you're like many people, breaking up can be so painful that it's only something people regret they never did at the end of a terrible, terrible marriage. Still, more often, the marriage was fine, just boring.

Even again still, for many of us, it isn't something we wait to do at the end of life, but something we do all the time to people we've led on, or drunkenly allowed to touch us. Whether it's something good gone bad, something bad gone super bad, or something good gone boring, there are some great and simple ways to let people know you want to break up.

Short Cuts and Guidelinesies to Breakin' Ups

1. You hire a lawyer. Everyone knows that if the lawyer of someone you're dating contacts you, your relationship is over. I'm not even sure if everyone knows that, but I guess it's probably the case. Right?

2. I imagine if you filled a large, black trash bag with dead fish and gave it to someone, they'd be weirded out. Then, you should be like, "It's over."

3. Shit under their pillow.

4. Never do it over e-mail. If you want to do it in writing, that's fine. But please, have the decency to write it on a napkin or something.

5. Never do it over the phone. This is also a no-no. Please, instead, either talk to them in person, or as I just suggested, just shit under their pillow. Seriously. It'll work. They *definitely* won't be all, "It was so cold—after all we've been through, he just shit under my pillow." They will be happy.

Your Love Quiz

Here is a brief quiz about love. This will both test what knowledge you've just absorbed and also show how you've grown as a person. Don't worry, if you don't do well, it means my test is flawed, not you. That's what you should tell yourself. Sometimes the mind needs to hide things from itself. This quiz may be one (maybe two *!!!!!*) of those things.

1. How important is love?
   a. *Very.*
   b. *Sort of.*
   c. *Very sort of.*

2. Is it okay to have an unrealistic fantasy of what love is?
   a. *Yes, it's where Heart Boners come from.* ▶

    b. *No! Hollywood creates such unrealistic expectations about love that many twenty-somethings are constantly alone and feel like something is wrong with them.*

    c. *All of the above and all of the below, man. Whatever, it's all good. (This answer is only available to hippies, awkward teens, and members of Fall Out Boy—whoever they are.)*

3. **What is the best way to tell someone you love them?**
    a. *Give them a meaningful gift that you make.*
    b. *Buy them a house or a horse, whichever is bigger.*
    c. *Fuck them for a long time and then bring them ice cream.*

4. **What is considered too many times to have been in love?**
    a. *8*
    b. *1209*
    c. *1 (Life is a bag of cold dirt).*

5. **How important is money in matters of love?**
    a. *Not at all.*
    b. *More then you think.*
    c. *A little. You need just enough to not steal VCRs (which are useless anyway) and climb out of fire escapes like they did in movies set in New York in the '80s.*

6. **Can you fall out of love?**
    a. *Yes.*
    b. *I think so.*
    c. *No! Love binds the soul, even into death! Otherwise the concept behind* The Mummy *starring Brendan Fraser wouldn't make sense.*

▶

7. Some people put blood or other gunk in potions to cast spells on people they love. Is that a good idea?
   a. *I don't think that's right.*
   b. *If it's the difference between experiencing an orgasm or not, then sure.*
   c. *Yuk!*

8. How do you know if you're in love?
   a. *You smile a lot in public places without noticing and it freaks people out.*
   b. *You get actual butterflies in your stomach and then throw up.*
   c. *You write a poem about someone and read it at your office talent show. Then try to commit suicide, but fail and live happily ever after.*

9. When you think about spending a special evening with the one you love, do you:
   a. *Pretend to excuse yourself to the bathroom for three hours (in your mind).*
   b. *Make a nice dinner and try to talk about having a family.*
   c. *Hire a prostitute as a "joke," but then suggest having a three-way. It works! Your relationship is great again and you didn't even have to have a kid!!!!! Awesome!!!!!*

Ca-Motherfuckin'-Reer, Ca-Motherfuckin'-Job, and Ca-Motherfuckin'-Business

"Sorry about your continent, but it's time to make money."

—from *Mr. Business Means Business*, Eugene Mirman's economic plan that rekindled Europe's economy after World War II

Some people seem to be born with the business gene. They look at an old table on the side of the road and do not see an old table (not because their vision is bad; that'll be covered in the chapter, "Why Some People Can't See Old Tables"); they instead see an *opportunity*. They don't see discarded furniture; they see a supply chain waiting to happen. By the way, supply chain is a real business term. Eight years ago, I ate the brain of Alan Greenspan (the one you know is actually a robot) and consumed all his knowledge. (Eating brains for knowledge is not as easy as it sounds, so don't do it unless you have training.)

At any given moment you stand at the threshold of opportunity, just a million dollars and a new idea away from having fifty million dollars and the kind of car a Poison groupie would let you punch her in the face to ride in. I will help you cross over that threshold and punch that groupie.

A warning: There are those who look at the triumphs of new industry and technology and get scared—generally it's big business, Saudi Arabia, and Mennonites. (They also fear women—so if you really want to piss them off, build a high-powered working-single-mom robot that delivers media in a new way. They'll hate it.)

There is always a fearful dinosaur guarding the gates of advancement—trying to eat the nerds responsible for break-throughs and their savvy venture capitalist pals.

It's an old tale whispered in the halls of industry. (What the fuck am I talking about?!) Radio, VCRs, and mix tapes all scared Hollywood bigwigs. Contrary to these fears, most of these new technologies made far more money than they lost. (Only now, with MP3s ruling the audio kingdom, are old media's fears realized.)

Obviously, business isn't about new technology (though that is a very good way to become very, very rich). It is about opportunity, ingenuity, salesmanship, and capital.

> *"To scare fear itself is very scary for fear."*
> —paraphrased by Eugene Mirman from Franklin Delano Roosevelt

The point is: Move forward—either with the help of old, rich men, or without. You are the pilot, and the market is your airplane/spaceship, depending on your level of ambition.

What Is a Business?

....

There is a difference between "work," "a job," and "business." This is obvious to anyone who knows the difference between words that aren't the same. From what I once heard about semiotics, language is a complicated lady covered in secret vaginas that each need attention.

We know this much for sure: Business is often a commercial enterprise that involves making and selling products, services, or ideas—sometimes the thing is fake, like the perception that you will be cool if you wear a certain sneaker or pee off a particular building. Sometimes the merchandise is very real—like a teriyaki chicken salad or a Toyota Corolla. Not to blow your mind, but imagine the profits from a teriyaki chicken salad that is *also* cool!! That is something that corporate money-mongers call branding. (The only object that doesn't fit any known business model is the Easy Button at Staples. What kind of person buys a functionless object of uncool branding is the topic for a study I plan to commission at Boring University, a place I'll found in 2011. Maybe I will put it in Belchertown, Massachusetts?)

Whether it's Adam and Eve's fault or not, we all have to make a living. You can choose to have a job working for "The Man." (That is a slang term that is appropriated from African-American culture and also other cultures where people are black but not originally from Africa and live in America. Obviously, there isn't a lot of money to be made from simply appropriating terms. However, in this chapter we will learn how to take goods and concepts from other cultures and make a huge profit off of them.)

Karl Marx would have you believe that wealthy people have

lots of power and exploit the poor. I'm not sure if that's true, but regardless, wouldn't it make sense for you to be one of the rich people? As long as you don't make things so unfair and bad that there is war, the answer is yes. But it is important to placate people with good health care, education, and women. And of course women are then placated with snacks, health care, and hats.

> *"Willpower can turn an idea into money, and money can turn an idea into power, and power, that can let you do almost anything—just ask the villains in* Die Hard 1 *through 4."*
>
> —Bruce Willis, to Eugene Mirman, trying to cover up for the fact that *Die Hard 2* is unwatchable

New Businesses
From Concept to Company to Fucking Rich

Find a hole in a market or neighborhood and fill it. That simple, mo-fo-bro.

Retail

This is probably the most common type of business. Some of these can be very big, like Macy's, or very small like a street vendor who sells dance mixes and cell phone accessories. The first thing you need to decide is what kind of store you'd like to open. Here are a few options:

1. A clothing boutique.

2. A specialty food store that has swing dancing on weekends.
3. A thrift/antique shop.
4. A chain of stores for tall people that sells non-tall-person-based items like pots and pans, jewelry, baseball cards, books, arts and crafts materials, etc. Potential slogan: "If you're tall, shop here."
5. A discount medical supply company for curious dabblers.

Now that you've picked a kind of store, pick a location. If you live in a town with strip malls, open it there. If not, then dedicate a floor of your house to your store. People love to go some place "cool" or "unique," and what is more unique than someone who sells medical supplies right out of their home?

The Service Industry

Restaurants

Going out to eat is one of history's great simple pleasures, except during the Paleolithic era, when it would have been dangerous. And probably Mesolithic, too. Otherwise, in almost every country, culture, and age, going out to eat is a delight and privilege. That's where you come in. Even though most restaurants and cafés are lucky to make around a 5 percent annual profit, you're going to open one that turns a 158 percent profit. How? By adding opium to your food. If you are too much of a pussy to do that, there is another way . . .

First, you have to figure out what kind of restaurant you want to open: regular, regular fancy, café, gourmet, chain, or ethnic. Every restaurant is a combination of one or more of those. If you can think of a restaurant that can't be put in those categories (1) it's not a restaurant, or (2) it's a terrible restaurant. Example: "Hey, Eugene, how about a restaurant that only serves hot bricks?" Yes, a rich enough person could open that in a country with lax public health laws, like Cambodia or Sweden Island. But I don't have time to explore all the bad restaurant opportunities wealthy people could make on foreign soil. This is about opening a restaurant in America (or one of its colonies —Canada, Europe, Guam, Japan, etc.).

Once you've decided what kind of restaurant you're opening (seafood or Asian fusion, I hope!!!), you'll need to name it. The name of a restaurant can make or break it. Here are some common names to avoid:

1. Ground Round (not a great name and already taken)
2. Chinese Blood Box
3. We're Racist!
4. Fat Guy's Uh-Oh Shack

As long as you avoid those names, your restaurant should be great.

There are two crucial things left: finding a hot location and hiring a trustworthy and polite (but sassy!) staff. For location, I recommend asking a gay person or a writer where they'd like to live and find a spot within a one-mile radius. (Make sure the area has not been in the process of gentrification for more than five years if it's a city, or that it is on top of a fancy mountain if it is a town.) The biggest mistake is asking a video artist or keyboard player (especially moog!) where they'd live. They'll recommend some crazy neighborhood filled with boarded up candy cane factories where way-too-quirky homeless vets live in converted elevators and forts. Trust me, you don't need that shit.

Hiring quality staff can be tricky. Before you hire someone, ask your gut if they seem unstable. Also, ask your gut if the person you are hiring is a white teenager with dreadlocks. One out of ten white teenagers with dreadlocks is a wonderful, hard-working employee. However, the other nine are mad at their upper-middle-class upbringings and give really long speeches about either jam bands or their favorite senator. Some good people to hire are (1) girls who just graduated from college with a humanities background (English, History, Sociology, etc.), (2) food snobs with tattoos, or (3) anyone in their thirties with a slightly shady past (an arrest for a bar fight, small-time drugs, or a general "I don't talk about my Navy days" attitude).

Last of all, it always helps to have a signature dish. This can be as simple as a delicious muffin with a gold coin inside, or as complicated as a steamed lobster stuffed with shrimp, crab, and mushrooms, baked, smothered in buttered duck paté, explained the process of taking GREs, shown Ken Burns's *The War*, pan-seared, told it was adopted, and finally served, two or three days later. (You have not tasted deliciousness until you try a lobster that has watched *The War*.)

> *"Let's party!"*
>
> —Eugene Mirman, March 20, 2003,
> accidentally at the start of the Iraq War

A Nightclub

A nightclub can be a lot of fun to own—if you don't get mixed up in drugs. Unlike many other businesses, nightclubs are really, really easy to run and are basically a printing press for money. There are only seven things (commonly referred to as the Seven Club-Mandments) you need to know/do/have:

1. A red velvet rope.
2. A bisexual man at the door keeping undesirables out.
3. Five million dollars to fight accusations of dealing GHB and Rohypnol out of the coatroom.
4. A DJ who is willing to fake his own death every night.
5. A back room for VIPs with a stripper's pole and a bidet.
6. Drinks that are twenty-five dollars and up.
7. Mashed potato bar with crazy fixin's (bacon, scallions, gorgonzola, baked cod, corn on the cob, wild boar, whole deep-fried rabbit, Quiznos Subs).

> *"I give you the tools, but what you build with them is up to you."*
>
> —Eugene Mirman, frustratedly speaking at a tool-presentation ceremony to bored teens in Chateauroux, France

Back in the mid-'90s, I was in France presenting underprivileged children with tools as part of an international organization I started called Shop Class for the French. Last year I found out that many of those students didn't speak English and never figured out how to use the tools I gave them. Most of those non-English speaking students became prostitutes or bus drivers. Even though I gave the French students actual tools, and to you I give only figurative ones, I hope that you understand me and use that knowledge to build a successful nightclub or restaurant. Good luck.

Various Service Jobs

There are also a lot of service jobs that are simpler than owning a business but very satisfying and can even sometimes be done from home.

1. Tutor.
2. Home decorator.
3. Owner of a store where parents can bring their twelve-year-old child to learn about reproduction from a nice Italian lady.
4. Software consultant.
5. Owner of a quirky, home-based copy shop where people pay to have sex instead of getting copies.

Game!

Make up your own career by picking one word from category A, one from category B, and one from D. I mean C. Let's go!

A	B	C
Clean	Corporate	Waiter
Master Class	Technophobic	Massage Therapist
Super Duper	Balls-Out	Dancer
Retarded	Software	Brand Analyst
Fancy	Rough	Lawyer
Level 8	Middle	Fucker
Commander	Sexist	Psychologist
Exotic	Death	Sales Associate

Agriculture

This is one of the oldest and most important fields in human civilization. Agriculture can be traced back to Thomas Jefferson. It can be traced back even further, too. That's just how old it is. If you seriously want to be in agriculture, whether it's your interest in a sustainable earth, or you want to grow poisonous vegetables to give permanent, debilitating diarrhea to an ex-lover, buy some land and get plantin'. The basics for farming are simple. All you need are the following things:

1. Land.
2. A slave. (Just kidding. That business model is now illegal.)
3. Seeds.

4. A rake.

5. Gumption.

6. A torn-up T-shirt revealing a sweaty, hairy chest.

7. A mule and some LSD to give that mule. (Trust me—a mule on acid is twice as effective.)

8. Something to till with.

9. A computer to Google *till* so you don't hurt yourself.

10. A giant corporation that is trying to push you off your land unjustly.

11. A shotgun and twenty-five thousand dollars to hire the A-Team.

12. A hot daughter or a hot farmhand.

A mule on LCD.

Manufacturing

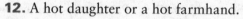

This is boring, but I'll still help you. Put on a suit and go to a bank and ask for forty thousand dollars. If they decline the loan, borrow forty thousand dollars from a relative and buy a building with some buddies near Arkansas. Then, pick either machine parts, sneakers, or whatever and make them. Next, you'll need to hire a porn star to fuck your product on camera. Upload that to the user section of CNN.com, if there is one. Within a week you should get orders from the buyers at Sears,

Costco, Caldor, Target, or Macy's. If they don't call, contact P. Diddy. He will know what to do.

> *"If your business is in the red, call the P. Diddy to get ahead."*
> — Eugene Mirman, from his inspirational corporate lecture series *I Imagine P. Diddy Knows How To Run a Business*

Internet and Software Startups

This is pretty much where all the big money is. If you were one of the lucky kids who got a PC Jr. or Apple IIc in 1985 and got heavily involved in the world of BBSs, Pascal, C++, and Logo, you already know this because you are reading this book from a helicopter that you can fly anywhere in the world and throw exotic fruit, steaks, and jewelry to Normals. (That's what you call humans with a net worth of less than five hundred million dollars.) You are so rich the law does not apply to you. You have so much money that when the police or FBI questions you about a crime you may or may not have committed, you write them a check for so much money that they kill themselves and still find it profitable. That is soooo cool!

Those of you who are just breaking into the world of high-tech start-ups have a lot to learn, but a lot to gain. What do you need to get going and get rich?

1. A product. You need to come up with software or some Web application that people really need (or think they need!!!!!!! Hahahaha!!! LOL!!! People, right?). Some examples are E*TRADE, an operating system like Windows, or an on-line application that creates 3-D models of your teachers and lets you see them naked doing chores. (You can use that if you want, no prob.)

2. A CEO. Every company needs a person (preferably a little girl, because they are the most cutthroat) who can follow through on a vision, raise capital, and inspire his/her employees.

3. Kickass programmers and IT team. Your software needs to be top-notch, A-game stuff. In software, there is room for two companies: the best and the biggest. There is no room for a third. So hire a bunch of misfit MIT dropouts and secure a dominant market share. If the programmers slack off, you can always scare them by showing a photograph from the future of the end of time. (Nerds are easily terrified by apocalyptic imagery.)

4. Marketing. Good news, you have a new application that is really something special. Guess what, no one knows about it. Why? Because you don't have a *marketing* department—you didn't think it was important. Well, it is. Why do you think Filemaker Pro is so popular? Because a team of marketing *wizards* (literally) told you to love it and buy it. I know, not the best example. But my gusto kind of proves its own point. (Shhhh . . . I don't think I'm right.)

5. A sales person. You'll need a great sales person. Personally, I recommend getting Harrison Ford. Who wouldn't buy a new online banking tool or whatever from that guy? He's awesome.

6. Capital. Everybody knows that the world runs on money. Just ask anybody. That's what they'll say. A few people may say love, but they are answering a different question that they've simply asked themselves, which is not fair.

Depending on the size of your start up, you'll need between one and ten million dollars. So, go find a venture capital firm and start selling.

You're almost ready. You can have two end-game business models: You can either sell your company to a bigger company

(Sony, Mickey D's, Billy Joel, etc.), or you can go public and IPO it. Taking a company public can be tricky, so make sure to hire some thugs to beat up anybody that gives you lip, like the feds or Morgan Stanley (if he's even a real person). You can also use snakes to scare people into buying your stock.

Either way, don't forget to "like wear a rubber in the shower," if you know what I mean, which you don't, because it's too complex. So to really *understand* this, buy my other book, *Eugene's Confusing Analogies, Explained!* (Do you see what I did there? I gave you 99 percent of the tools you needed and then offered the last 1 percent for a fee. That is World-Class Grandmaster Salesmanship.)

Get-Rich-Quick Schemes

The easiest way to get rich fast nowadays is Internet spam. I personally find it unpleasant, but that's where the quick cash is. You should create an e-mail spam campaign that offers idiots a chance to buy a cream that grants them ten wishes. If a person orders Wish Cream through the mail, then it's okay that you tricked them. If you are feeling bold, make the spam for a cream that simply makes their wishes longer.

Inventors

You're my favorite. I love an inventor. A good inventor is like a good woman; they will challenge you and please you. Other things that are like a good woman: a skyscraper, a very expensive car, a bad woman (This one is more literal.)

There are three important rules to being a successful inventor:

1. Do not fall for the ads on television that try to lure you into giving up your idea in exchange for your paying them. That is a very, very bad deal. Do not sign anything you understand poorly, unless you are very broke or the man you are talking to is from the Army and is threatening you.

2. Do not invent something that could be written into a Rick Moranis vehicle as a silly invention. Always ask yourself, "Is this invention too Rick Moranis for the real world?"

3. Listen to your heart and build, my friend, build—unless the invention fits under rule two; then stop building and start over.

For inventors who are stuck and can't think of something to invent, here are a few suggestions:

1. An edible book that you read by eating.

2. A machine that tells women they are pretty instead of you. (Good one, me!!!!)

3. A train that takes meatheads, snobby upper-class ladies, and racists to Mexico and leaves them there to walk back. Not really an invention, but it would cheer a lot of people up.

4. A sword that is made of laser (like the one in the movie *Star Wars: The Phantom Menace*).

5. A room where couples enter, yell their grievances, and then leave happy, and maybe pregnant. (Right now all we have are New Year's parties and hotel rooms.)

6. An indestructible shirt that is fun at parties. (People can throw fire at it, shoot it, and smash it with a tire iron, and the person wearing it laughs and then raises his drink in the air and goes, "Cheers!")

7. A glove that makes it so that men and women don't have to go to the bathroom. This will solve some of the current fears of space travel.

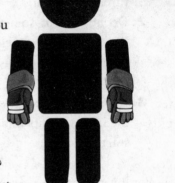

I HAVEN'T PEED IN YEARS!

8. A body wash that makes you lose weight.

9. A gun that shoots pain at people from up to half a mile away. Oh, oops. Never mind. The Army already built that. Maybe you could make it portable?

10. A very heavy hat you can put on religious extremists that makes them go to sleep.

Temping
....

Temping is a rite of passage for anybody interested in a career in entertainment. It's also a great way to explore possible professions, like law and finance (but not medicine—unless you become a doctor of partying, but that does not count as a job), or, it can help you lead the dead-end life you've dreamed of since you saw *Office Space*.

Any temp job can be divided into one of two things: random bullshit job, and breaking-into-a-new-career job. Depending on your interests and personality, these could be totally different job experiences, but at the same company.

> **"Temping is something I wouldn't wish on a homosexual."**
> —Eugene Mirman, if he were a conservative religious leader with heart

Random Bullshit Jobs

In Boston, after college, I temped at Fidelity Investments for several months. My direct boss was a good guy, but the rest of the company seemed shitty. Both law and investment firms are feudal in nature and seem to lack the instinct to treat all employees like people rather than fourteen-dollar-an-hour hookers with no future or teeth. My job was to answer questions about people's accounts and stocks, etc., and then forward them on to traders if they wanted to buy or sell.

It was fun sometimes. I'd change the screensavers of all the computers around me to say POOPMONKEY. That was fun. Another time, we were manning the phones and watching MSNBC waiting to hear whether Alan Greenspan was going to lower the interest rate. Finally, he came on television and announced that he would. I stood up in the large room of about four hundred people and, at the top on my lungs, screamed *"Nooooooo!!!!"* (Even though everyone was excited for it and thought it would be good for the economy.)

When I moved to New York, I got a temp job at Weil, Gotshal & Manges, a law firm that may be the third biggest in the world (or so). They are

> **"A resentful staff is a good staff."**
> —Eugene Mirman, from his book, *How To Be A Terrible Company*

gigantic. (At the time I worked there, their clients included Enron, WorldCom, and the Taliban—that last one is not true and is a mean-spirited joke. Sorry, Mr. Gotshal.) Aside from the periodic phone calls I'd get from my agency asking me to dress "more professionally" (I used to wear a silver onesie with my dick out all the time), this place was all right. Just kidding—it was terrible. My job here was to be a floating secretary. When a lawyer's secretary was sick or on vacation, I would fill in. It was exactly as fun as it sounds, no more, no less.

Once, I was in the elevator (a metal box that goes up and down a building, if you are just starting the book here and are from another world). I was wearing a badge around my neck (as everyone was required to), with my name, a photo (of me, not Al Sharpton—oh, well), and in large letters it said TEMPORARY. In the elevator with me were two secretaries, one cunty, one probably nice. The cunty one looked at me and my badge and then said to the other secretary, "How many temps do we need?" There were only three of us in the elevator. Later, when she was on vacation, I subbed for her and hid fifty live squirrels in her desk. That's not true. I never gave in to the petty world of the Secretary Wars.

Throughout my years temping I learned a lot of survival skills at these cutthroat companies. For instance, did you know that architecture firms have their own system of filing things and that you shouldn't work there for more than one day? I do. Obviously, assess your situation and do what you feel is right, but here are some suggestions to make the best of your temp job:

1. Bring everyone you work with a present on the last day of your first week. *Warning:* Do not give blood wontons wrapped in human skin. (Last time I take a gift idea from playing a metal record backwards.)
2. Try to steal as much stuff as you can and make fun of the people who are in charge.

3. Invite everyone for drinks after work and try to seduce them with unlimited power. Obviously, you'll need a Cosmic Cube.
4. Pretend every day is Bring a Coyote to Work Day.
5. Pick a person and tear their life apart. It is better to pick someone with power who will not see it coming.

> *"A new job is like a new glove. You are excited, but it's just a glove. Still, maybe it will fit well?"*
>
> —Eugene Mirman, talking to a friend who only understands things in terms of gloves

From Temp to Career

Did you know that Roger Smith of General Motors started as a temp? Alfred Hitchcock, before he was a filmmaker, temped on the set of his own movie! It's true. So if you're serious about a career, temping is a good way to get in the door. Another way is to just show up, walk around, pick a desk, and start doing stuff. Maybe even pretend to be in charge? It's fun, but it's a risky road.

Less risky is to get a temp job in a field you want to work in. I recommend trying hard, impressing your bosses, and not stealing (too much). If this job means a lot to you, try to marry the owner's son or daughter. If the movies *My Boss's Daughter* and *In Good Company* are even a little true, your life is about to be great.

> *"It isn't about the truth; it's about wearing a lie well."*
>
> —Eugene Mirman, on a conference call with Britney Spears's son Sean, trying to help him mold his public persona

Public Relations and Image
···

Some PR is about getting information about a great product or thingy out to the people who would enjoy it, while other PR is about creating a web of lies that conceals the fact that your company harnesses the energy produced by rape and uses it to make a chemical that kills forests for fun. Either way, you're going to need it.

Branding
··············

Some companies pay trillions of dollars to be "cool." (Well, the Army does.) That's a lot of money, and most companies don't even have half that. I offer a *quick fix*: For a hundred thousand dollars, if anyone asks me, I will tell them your product is cool. I'll make people think anything from your stupid soda is "liberating" and "rad" (Mountain Dew?) to turning a murder at your office into "cachet." You can also do it on your own, of course. I was just trying to become very rich quickly.

The same way that giant snack and soda companies associate themselves with cool things, so should you. If you have the money to place your product on a popular teen show, do it (even if your product is gross—like Urine Pillow).

The world is moving from simple product placement, like people wearing an Apple computer in a porn film, to people placement, where you, the person who wants to be cool, gets to place yourself inconspicuously on a television show. Instead of kids sitting on a bed eating Doritos in their dorm room, it'll be two kids sitting on *you*, eating Doritos in their dorm room. And when people see you at parties, they'll be like, "Hey, were you the guy they sat on in *The OC*?" Swoosh! You did it. You're "hot."

Advertising

....

It's dead, don't bother. I'm kidding. Only the thirty-second spot is dead. You can still put up billboards and buy ads in magazines. Just make them flashy and make sure to quote the president about your product. Having the president say he likes something can really make it sell. (Remember the Iraq War? Do you have any idea how unpopular that war would have been if the president never said he liked it?)

Work and Pleasure
Outings, Team Building, Work Parties
....

Work Friends

Work friends can become your real friends, because of how much you have in common, in both your day-to-day lives and from whatever otherworldly forces brought you to the same workplace. In some instances, you may even marry a work friend, like the members of Fleetwood Mac did.

Because people are always looking for ways to connect with each other, you'll be tempted to share too much, too quickly with colleagues. Unless you are a hopeless romantic about your job (which would be weird), take it slow. There is no reason to get to third base on your first date of work. (I hope you read the word date slower than the other words.)

Don't go blabbing about your family's dysfunction or your sketchy military past right away. (There is nothing more un-comfortable than sharing a CIA death-squad secret with the one person you like at work and then having to kill them two weeks later because they turn out to be untrustworthy and flaky.)

Keep it friendly but professional for the first month. You don't want the nickname Chatty and Upsetting Francis (gender-neutral name alert!). Then, seven weeks into the job, you get into a groove and start to feel settled—it's sharing time! Maybe right before a strategy meeting or in the elevator on your way to lunch, open up a little, like, "I can't stop thinking about my mortality. You?" or "I've had some bad memories of a creepy teacher resurface, but there's a lot of debate on whether you can trust them."

So, have fun, keep it semi-professional, and give it a few months before you tell everyone your secret plan to restore the glory of the Roman Empire.

After-Work Drinks

Two rules: Have fun and don't say anything that comes off as unabashedly bigoted.

Hooking Up with Coworkers

Many relationships, even marriages, start at work. Although the government has a lot of rules about unwanted sexual advances, there are even more rules about wanted sexual advances—though these are not enforced by the executive branch, but by social structures. The bottom line is, if you hook up more than three times with a colleague, you will either have a serious relationship, or one of you will leave your job if things go bad within a year. So, depending on how much you like the person/are horny, it may be worth it. Have fun, and don't get herpes! (There is nothing worse than being know as "That account manager with herpes.")

Office Parties

All right, you've earned it. You know what to do—go score some acid, Ecstasy, or dust, give it out, take some yourself, but most of all, *cut loose!* It's time to *un-wind* (pronounced "un-wine-d," not "un-win-d," because then it would have something to do with being gassy and that would ruin your party).

Sexual Harassment:
Avoidin' Doin' It, Dealin' with Gettin' It
(Funk Song Inspiration Alert! Turn That Subhead into a Hit)

Everybody faces unwanted sexual advances (especially Catholic children—because of the whole priest thing!!!!!!!!!!!!!
!!
!!
!!
!!
!!
!!
!!
!!
!!
!!
!!

!!
!!!!!!!!!!!!).

Anyway. . .

Hey, guess what? It's not 1955, so, cut the shit, jerk-off. It makes people uncomfortable when you make jokes about your dong at a finance meeting or point at people's private parts.

I know—but what about the video of a lady opening a champagne bottle in her doodle-spot? It's really funny and I want to show it to a girl I work with that's like a guy's girl (even though I do want to sleep with her). Well, you can show it to her, but if she doesn't like it and you get fired, you have to accept it and not whine to your parents about it when you move back in.

Everyone knows that there is an invisible line between wanted and unwanted sexual advances. The best way to tell if your advances are unwanted is to ask yourself, "When I make a sexual comment to my colleague, does he/she laugh uncomfortably? Are they being polite because of our power dynamic?" If the answer is yes, I'm sorry, but you have to stop. Okay?

If you don't, then it is only fair that I inform you that the government (at least in Vermont) has been working on a machine that would act as a deterrent to sexual harassment. Inspired by the Green movement, this machine is powered by sunlight. What it does is burrow into your ass, dig through your intestines into your brain, and yell "Cut it out" each time you say something lewd at work. So far the results are less than spectacular. The machine has no effect on the only people tested—Taco Bell employees.

If you are the victim of sexual harassment and feel like you have nowhere to turn (because you are being harassed in a small space like a closet—just kidding, trying to lighten the mood), take a deep breath and get your Justice Spoon ready, because you are about to *dish out* big, cold balls of mint justice!

You'll need around five hundred dollars or good credit to do this. Go to your local spy store (there probably is one in or near your town) or go online and buy a spy camera button. Then tape whoever is bugging you at work, and after about a week you should have enough evidence to get a two hundred and fifty thousand dollar settlement. Remember to turn the bug off before you fuck anyone in the copy room—it will go against your credibility. Good luck. If things are really overwhelming and you need to talk, you can give me a call at 347-273-2044. (I just broke not the third or fourth wall, but the fifth wall by giving you a phone number where can reach me. I am really there for you. That is so cool of me. But, sadly, it's not as modest of me as it is noble.)

Getting Away with It (Don't Do It)

Come on buddy, don't do it—it's wrong. But if you must, try to make everything harassing you say have a double meaning. That way, if someone ever pressed charges, you won't get in trouble for saying, "Is there a fruit stand nearby? I want to get some melons." Sexual harassment? No. All I heard was a vegetarian looking for a healthy snack.

Kitchen/Watercooler Etiquette

Watercooler chitchat, or what is now more commonly kitchenette chitchat, is a nice way to break up your day. Depending on who you're talking to, it's a fun time-waster, an excruciating lesson about how to build a canoe, or a cute flirtation. A safe way to go is to keep the conversation to gossip at the office. Everyone likes to point at a random colleague and then talk about their secrets. It's super fun.

If you don't really know the person well, you are allowed to name a television show you saw recently or say one thing about your weekend, though nobody really cares—unless you banged a griffin; then spill the beans. What's it like to fuck a half-lion, half-eagle creature? Do tell.

Of course, to avoid getting stuck in that convo with someone you dislike or feel uncomfortable around, don't be passive, be proactive. Do not let them direct your interaction on their terms, do it on yours. Ask a Misdirection Question—something too difficult to answer quickly—e.g., "What's Congress up to?" or "You ever learn any cool science?" When you ask the question, don't make eye contact, keep moving and get out of there. Do not wait for a response and deny ever asking it. Repeat these actions until you are never again spoken to by that individual (about four times).

Photocopying Your Boobs

This is not appropriate. In the 1960s, it may have been a great way to find a husband, but in the modern day, it's considered classless, I am told. (I used to do it all the time at my old job.) Sadly, even some of the most harmless photocopying pranks today end in suicide.

There you have it. You're ready for business—unless you want to be a rock star or a playwright. Then there is a lot to learn. . .

The Entertainment Industry

The Business of the Arts

> **"Entertainment is business:**
> **the business of fucking art in the face."**

—Eugene Mirman, at a private dinner at the Rustic Oak restaurant
in North Haven, Connecticut, with Robert McKee and Billy Wilder

Humanity has long idolized entertainment and the arts. Ancient Greeks would masturbate in amphitheaters to Homer's *Iliad* out of respect. (Public masturbation as an expression of approval became frowned upon only in 1865, at the end of the American Civil War.) Philosophers and kings regarded art as the height of human accomplishment. Schopenhauer thought art (not entertainment, but they are so intertwined) was one of the few things that could break through the world of illusion that we all live in. (He was wrong—it was Go-GURT, the portable yogurt. Wait, how was yogurt not portable before?)

Where art ends and entertainment begins, where fame begins and spectacle ends, are not for me to judge. I'm just here to help you work in this field. What you do with your success and riches is up to you. Whether you "sell out" or remain "true of heart" is for you to decide.

Every year, *People* magazine votes for the world's hundred sexiest men alive, and they're all celebrities. Nobody ever bothers to fly to Ottawa or Miami and see if there is someone sexier than George Clooney. What's my point? To be honest, I forget. To lie, however, it's that you can become a celebrity and be invited into the fast-paced world of magazine glitz. (Plus, there will be lots of free jeans and digital cameras in it for you.)

What to Do with Your Fine Arts Degree in Today's Capitalist World

Congratulations! You have a degree in painting, photography, graphic design, dance, or some other parent-worrying field. However, because blue-collar work is being replaced by robots (who will soon be replaced by people-slaves), and medical jobs are being shipped overseas to Vietnam and Nepal, creative white-collar jobs are at an all-time high (except in dance, of course).

Did you know that you can work at almost any type of company with a fine arts degree? It's true; just e-mail them.

Make a resume and write a cover letter. Don't know what to say in the cover letter? No problem. You can just use one I've written for you:

Dear [Insert company name and addressee here.],

My name is Shonali Bhatnagar [Make sure to introduce yourself as an Indian lady. Once hired, you can reveal who you really are.] and I recently gradu-

ated from [your university] with a degree in [whatever useless crap—kidding—you majored in]. I am great at [things you are great at]. I also speak French, Spanish, and Mandarin, which in today's global economy is very important.

I am a very hard worker and if you hire me you won't regret it—unless you cross me; then I will destroy you (and all life on earth).

In conclusion, I would be a great addition to your company. Cool? Cool.

Sincerely,
Shonali Bhatnagar

P.S. I have been programmed to kill since the age of five.

Don't know who to contact? Don't worry. I'll start you off with a few places to reach out to:

Subway Restaurants. E-mail resume and cover letter to comments@subway.com. (It's not human recourses, but I'm sure it will reach them.)

Atlas Copco Drilling Solutions. (I have no idea what they do. I imagine it has to do with drilling.) E-mail resume and cover letter to drill.resumes@us.atlascopco.com.

Michigan State University. E-mail resume and cover letter to staffingservices@hr.msu.edu. (You can help college kids discover their bodies, though they will deny that in the job description.)

Mental Health Association of San Francisco. Fax resume and cover letter to: 415-421-2928. I bet this is a fun place. (Sorry, no e-mail.)

Hop-a-Jet Worldwide Jet Charter Inc. E-mail resume and cover letter to VMcfarland@soflajc.com. Make sure you have an idea of what you could do there, since I think you need a pilot's license to fly a plane. Even a terrorist needs part of one, so that's pretty strict.

"Rock and roll is just like any job, except it is much better in many, many ways."

—Eugene Mirman, explaining to Don Henley what makes his life choices special in a private counseling session that has been erased from Mr. Henley's mind

Rock and Roll
Going from "We Need a Drummer" to "I'm in an Awesome Somewhat Popular Band"

Forming the Band

Get a lead singer and guitarist. (It can be the same person.) Next, find a Jew to help with the rest. Most Jews have access to files of local drummers, bassists, keyboardists, etc. You're all set.

Don't forget to all have similar influences (excluding Canned

Heat—never allow more than one fan of Canned Heat in your band). It's also good to have some friction, so consider hooking up with each other's spouses.

Naming Your Band

This can often take months, even years. It's too bad Journey is taken, because that would've been a cool name for your band. And it really bites that Minnie Driver performs under her own name—so that's also out of the question, unless you are totally determined, in which case you can be Minnie Driver UK. The upside is you may benefit from her name recognition. (My band Led Zeppelin UK—not to be confused with the British band Led Zeppelin—sells tons of records.)

Essentially, there are three kinds of names for a band: a *the*-based name (the Shins, the Soft Boys, the Clash), a phrase (Clap Your Hands Say Yeah, Death From Above 1979), or a choice word or two (Phish, Arctic Monkeys, Weezer).

Here are three rules for how to pick your own band name:

1. What kind of music do you play?
2. Do you want to party?
3. See rule one! (That would have worked better if rule one sounded tougher.)

Your band is probably a cross between R.E.M., Lyle Lovett, and Arcade Fire, so you'll want to call yourselves one of the following things: Three's Company; Lips, Tits, and Wind; Donahue!; or the Guy Whose Face Ate Sex.

However, if you have a different sound or none of those names work for you, here's a fun game you can play to name your band. Simply pick a word each from column A, B, and C, and you'll have a band name on par with the Rolling Stones or Blink 182.

A	B	C
The	Suck-Suck	Go-Getter Bunch
Burned	German	Dork Association
Ethnic	Shazam-tastic	Sex Fiends 2025
Young	Wannabe	Whoa! Whoa! Whoa! Slow Down!
Asshole	Throw Your Junk at the Sun	Child Stars
Sexed Up	Missing	Swordsmen
Extinct	Multicultural	Meth Fuck Ups
Cheesy	Special Ed	2121
Drunk	Pissed Off	Kings

Obviously, play around. Take two from column A and one from C, or whatever. It's a free country (unless you are reading this in Syria—then only pick one from each category; I don't want you put to death for getting creative with band names). Finally, if you have the biggest balls in the world and want to be the hardest rocking, most indie, difficult-to-say band, use everything and become: The Suck-Suck Go-Getter Bunch Burned German Dork Association Ethnic Shazam-tastic Sex Fiends 2025 Young Wannabe Whoa! Whoa! Whoa! Slow Down! Asshole Throw Your Junk at the Sun Child Stars Sexed Up Missing Swordsmen Extinct Multicultural Meth Fuck Ups Cheesy Special Ed 2121 Drunk Pissed Off Kings. Now that's a band that rocks, I bet.

> *"A vibe is more than just a groove."*
>
> —Eugene Mirman, drunk one night with George Clinton,
> just chilling out and sharing

Getting a Vibe

First thing you need is a vibe. What's a vibe? In my 1992 bestselling treatise on Vibe, *Stages On Vibe's Way*, I wrote, "Vibe can only be understood backwards, but it must be vibed forward." It's so crazy that I'm still so right more than fifteen years later!

It is very easy to look at a band—the Doors, the Strokes, Death Cab For Cutie, even the fragile Cat Power—and know their vibe. However, it is much harder to create the vibe. Here are some easy ways to establish a vibe:

1. Get a band look—either all wear pressed suites or dungarees, etc. Maybe a stupid hat that says "Reagan"?
2. When performing live, go balls out. Don't hold back. Really show your fans you're having a good time.
3. Sometimes act real pissy when you take your van to the car wash.
4. Get drunk and save a teenage girl from a burning car in Holland. (Do not set the car on fire yourself, please.) Then tell U2's the Edge (or Adam Clayton, if you have no other option) and have him bring it up at the Thursday cocktail party with Stereogum, Gawker, Salon, Pitchfork, etc. (There is a giant meeting of all the online superpowers the first Thursday of every month at Beauty Bar in New York.)

5. Try to get in a fight at a bar where you kill a white supremacist family in self-defense. This will set a really sweet vibe.

6. Cry as much as you can at restaurants.

7. Add masturbation to your live show. Also, consider bringing someone from the audience on stage and singing a song to their butt.

8. Train with swords, learn bujutsu, and add a demonstration of Japanese martial arts to your live show. (Only do this if you get very good—nobody wants to see a kick-ass band flub their show because of poor swordsmanship.)

9. Before each show, steal an arm from a funeral home and throw it into the audience.

10. Give yourselves a theme. Maybe dress up like the characters from *Star Trek*, *The Brady Bunch*, or *The McLaughlin Group*? Perhaps you are all displaced Iraqis? Whatever you do, make it clear, and have fun with it.

Before each show, steal an arm from a funeral home and throw it into the audience.

Live Show

If you're a quiet band, try to seem upset all the time—especially the trumpet player. (I know—now you have to find a trumpet player. It's worth it; trust me.) If you are loud, play so hard that you electrocute yourself when you step into a pool of your own sweat.

Finding a Label

Go on the Internet and find a list of every label. Then call each one asking what they look for in a new band. Most will tell you to have a unique sound. That's when you go, "Damn, yes! We have a unique sound! More—we have a vibe. We all wear suits, and here's a blog about a girl we saved from a burning car in Holland." They'll go, "Consider yourself signed!"

On the off chance that telling a label you have a vibe doesn't work, you should record a demo that really kicks ass, and you should also be an unstoppable live act. Tour for about two years and you'll get signed. The label may suck, but that topic's for my next book, *Leaving a Shitty Label That Signed You Because of Your Vibe*.

Industry secret: More indie labels listen to unsolicited stuff than you think. Still, you should quit any full-time day job for at least two years and act like the band is your only way to survive. That's what Metallica and Mötley Crüe did, along with thousands of bands you've never heard of. It's worth a shot.

Self-Releasing Your Album

If Radiohead can do it, so can you. That's what you should tell yourself every morning. Go for it, bro. Go for it.

The Internet: How to Harness the Power and Reach of New Media

Make a music video of all your friends fighting in a forest with animals. Make sure the animals are dangerous, but not too dangerous. So no one gets seriously hurt. Put that footage to your catchiest song and post it on YouTube. Then just wait. I forgot to add that everyone (including the animals) should be in their underwear.

Publicists

This is probably the most important thing to have that you don't think is important, because you are retarded and think that publicists aren't cool or something. Here's an actual conversation that happened at the beginning of a very, very popular band's career. (See if you can guess the band.)

Bass guitarist: We should get a publicist to promote our first single and upcoming tour.

Rhythm guitarist: No! Publicists are lie-mongers and truth-rapists! No way, bloke! [*That's right, this band is British.*]

Bass guitarist: But some publicists have forged strong bonds with journalists over many years.

Rhythm guitarist: I don't want to pay a lie-maker to make lies for me.

Drummer: You're both right. I want to be true to the R & B spirit that inspired us, but I'd love to get our music out there.

Rhythm guitarist: I don't know. . .

Bass guitarist: Look, maybe not in Liverpool, but in London there are some great publicists.

Rhythm guitarist: We're getting nowhere. This is exhausting. Let's all kill ourselves.

Drummer: Fine.

Bass guitarist: Agreed.

George Harrison: I'm out. I have a three-way at the Cavern tonight. Can I keep the band name?

Oh my God! That was the Beatles! Luckily for us, the Beatles did not kill themselves that night. Instead, they hired a publicist and became history's greatest rock band. That could sort of maybe be you, kind of.

> *"No more pantsuits from the future, got it?"*
>
> —Eugene Mirman, warning My Chemical Romance at a Starbucks that their look is approaching self-parody

The Benefits and Dangers of Super Cool
Rad Clothes and Avoiding a Douche Bag Look

An outfit can help define you. Clothes protect you from the elements, but they're also a reflection of your character. They send a message to let people know that you are sexy, dangerous, or even insane. But if your clothes stray too far from practical, you'll need to have the pizzazz of David Bowie or Madonna, or you will be teased and discarded by the world around you (right, MC Hammer and Cinderella?).

The main thing to avoid is looking like you're (1) trying too hard to look cool, or (2) on a reality dare show where the members of Poison compete with each other to dress you (especially if the winner was trying way too hard).

Look, as long as you have rock and roll in your heart, your pants and frilly shirt will follow. I'll just say the best bands dress cool, but not so cool you're mad at them. Here's a good rule of thumb: Think of five people from different parts of your life (friends, parents, exes, old teachers, musicians)—if more than three of them were to see what you're wearing and think to themselves, "Oh, shit! Call 911! Someone's OD'd on crazy pants and space boots, plus their torso has been mangled by a homemade leather-bomb!", at least change your top.

However, have fun. Look sexy. But don't overdo it. If Drew Barrymore looks good in it, you might not.

Going from Indie to Mainstream

You'll need to build up a solid fan base who won't abandon you when uncool people (that's where all the money is) start to like you. People love to think that a band is their secret that they get to die with. However, most bands want to share their music with a larger audience and get rich, fuck fans, crash jets into the desert, eat tons of sea creatures, ride horses in a mall—you know, rock and roll shit.

Once you know that a large group of fans won't betray you, plan a tour called the Sears Tour. That's right—try to play outside of every Sears in America, whether you have permission or not. Once word gets out that you are in cahoots with Sears, people will give you all their money and attention. It's that simple. Obviously, if another band does the Sears Tour, it doesn't matter. You can do it, too. If you feel guilty doing the same thing, you can do a Barney's tour. It will be a lot easier, and the people who shop there are so rich they may give you your own radio station.

The Danger of Nu-Metal's Flirtation with Nu-Marketing: A Warning

Nu-metal bands: Be careful. I know it can be hard, and success sometimes seems so close. But do not betray yourself—or you will turn into a boy band that was not put together by a savvy, pedophilic businessman, but is the product of artistic self-betrayal, cheap Chianti, and the inability to remain metal.

I (and many others) get a lot of ridiculous MySpace messages from nu-metal bands that sing about death, skulls, loneliness, mutilation, and general blood-spurting/puke-eating stuff wishing me a happy birthday.

Fact: It is not metal to wish a stranger through the Internet a happy birthday. It just isn't. You have to live like you are hanging out with Black Sabbath most of the time. Then ask yourself, "Is what I'm doing metal enough for Ozzy Osbourne to piss in my mouth?" It isn't if you're sending birthday greetings to strangers or paying a twenty-year-old girl to send flirty e-mails about your death-rock. (Do not become the Macy's gift card comment equivalent of metal.) Or worse, they send e-mails about how much they "*rock!*" Even more applicable than it is to literature, metal's maxim is also "Show, don't tell."

If you want to go on the street in your torn leather pants and hand a flyer to a slut, you go right ahead—that's metal. Hiring a girl (*even* if it's Sigourney Weaver) to send e-mails to random people that mimic the marketing strategy of ringtone companies is not metal, and your band should be put to death (the obvious punishment for betraying the Devil-God of Metal—which on earth is manifested in the physical form of Scott Ian's goatee).

Worship me, human! Or I will lock up all the pussy in the world!

All I ask is that if you have a metal band, you act metal. That means: drugs, liquor, pussy, fighting a wolf with one of those keyboard-guitar things, etc.—but not fakety-fake marketing that makes you as metal as a Warrant cover band on a VH-1 reality show called *Celebrity Hair-Metal Cuddle Party Challenge*.

To help guide you, here is the motto of the Metal Code of Metal Ethics:

Fuck it, drink it, fuck it, eat it, fuck it again.

Anything outside that is a lie.

Becoming a Successful (but Not Necessarily Good) Writer

••

Writers are the romantics of any generation, often creating the myths that become our culture. Everyone from Jean-Claude Van Damme to George Orwell to Jenny Craig uses writing in their lives. Even Jewel wrote a book of poems once. (She apologized for it later.)

Through willpower and a hint of talent, you can become a journalist, a screenwriter, a books writer (fiction *and* nonfiction), an ad-man (you'll need hormone shots if you're a lady), or a boring, boring poet. (In poetry's defense, it isn't the writing of it that is a problem, but the reading aloud that has taken so many lives. And the not calling it lyrics and putting it to awesome music part.)

First thing you need to do is figure out what you want to write. If you want to write a book or screenplay, you'll need to set a schedule. Every morning or evening, brew a cup of tea and write for one hour. If you would like to finish it before your life is up, maybe write for a few hours.

If you want to write a blog or nonfiction piece about your father, then you'll need a bottle of whiskey and some emotional baggage. Once you feel buzzed, start writing. Let it all out. Reread it the next morning to make sure you wrote beautiful things with your heart, and not jumbled, angry nonsense. Then press "publish."

> *"To be a writer you must write, but to be a waiter, you mustn't wait."*
>
> —Eugene Mirman, from his book *Sounds Like I'm Making a Point*

Many writers, after getting their undergraduate degree, ask themselves, "Should I go to Iowa (or some other university) for my master's?" Probably not. Some people go to grad school for writing, but you don't have to. Because, like, you have so much inside you that needs to come out. Plus, nows-a-day there are edit people with fixy buttons to make everything read right. On the other hand, the opposite point.

Visual Arts (or Simply "Art")

Painting and Photography (No Longer Just for Pretty Ladies and Effeminate Dudes!)

Painting, photography, and collage are all wonderful media. Painting is one of the oldest art forms, since it mostly involved figuring out how to keep a color in one place for a long time. So, there's a lot of history there. Go to the store and buy some supplies. The first time I did that, a homeless man gave me fifteen minutes of advice about painting. He told me to stretch my own canvas and to read the *New York Times* Sunday section to stay on top of what is happening. The homeless know art, so listen to them. Then put your art online and wait.

Collage: The Art of the Cut and Paste

Collage is more of a craft than an art form or profession. However, if you're really good, Neiman Marcus may hire you to do a display. Or if you're really attractive, some old person may pay you to live in their home and make them collages. They are probably doing it because of how attractive you are, but still, you get to work in the medium you love.

Good luck finding a collage agent—they don't exist. Unless you become one, and then your clients can be kids and tweens, asshole. Sorry to lash out; a close friend died in a collage. He was going to be the next president—of collage. I think that about wraps up my jokes about collage. Good luck, friend.

Become a Film Auteur
....

Film can be a rough business, but with all the advances in technology, it's become easy to become a filmmaker. The hard part is to become a filmmaker that makes films using other people's money. That's the real challenge.

To be a filmmaker, you mostly need to know or have the following things:

1. A video camera (preferably three-chip, though some say one large chip is better). Obviously, you can have a 35-millimeter camera, but most likely if you do, you are a filmmaker and I'd like you to stop reading my half-truths about film.
2. You need to know or have heard of storyboards. You don't need to use them, but you need to be aware of them.
3. A computer you can edit on—probably a tricked-out Mac. (Dear Apple Inc.: As you know, advertising is changing, and the way to get your products out there is through product placement. Though we have no sponsorship deal, could you please send me twenty-five thousand dollars—*not* greedy alert!—and some new hardware as a thank-you. Thank you.)
4. Balls and a vision.

5. A bottle of whiskey and a gritty world view.
6. A knack for either bringing out emotions in actors or writing dialogue for people who are not your race, gender, or class. Here is an example: two gang members, one, a black youth, the other, a fucked-up older white dude, are hanging out on the streets of downtown Chelmsford, Massachusetts in 1986. Try to figure out who is who:

Hanky: It pisses me off that the Police broke up. It's downright wicked un-shit-tastic.
Jake: Agreed, friend. Demz da breaks.
Hanky: Don't tell our other gang-member friends, but I was at a house party at the owner of Filene's Basement's house, and I went down on Molly Ringwald in the basement of this house party.
Jake: Whoa! That's so awesome. But no prob, chief. My lips are like a sewed up goat's asshole— tight, sealed, and mysterious. [*Pause.*] Wanna go to Dunks and jack some jelly do'noes?
Hanky: Yes, motherfucker. We can use my sword.
Jake: Yes, my black friend! High five!

[They high-five up high and down low.]

As you can see, it's not easy writing dialogue that is an accurate snapshot of history, but anyone can do it, given enough time and encouragement. Through my vivid words, we all got in a car and drove about four and a half hours north of Bernhard Goetz's mid-'80s.

All you have to do is think of yourself as the high-speed bus driver of a story. The road is images, dialogue, and sounds, and you've got to get everyone home safely, because there are fire-breathing rape vultures trying to prevent you from telling your great story with strong characters that make any sense. So bring an idea-rifle to blast the rape vultures out of the sky.

Also, a lot of people seem to enjoy taking Robert McKee's story seminar. Or you can just buy his book. Or watch a lot of classic movies.

Installation Artist (Also Called Fake Room Artist)

I'll be honest, I don't really know what to suggest. I guess erect a bunch of crazy, giant sculptures in public places in Europe at night without permission and then take pictures of them and send those photos to major museums and malls in college towns. I bet that will work.

Getting an Agent

For most of the jobs in the arts, you'll need an agent. The best way to get one is to put a sign up at a Laundromat that says, "Agent wanted—must tell me I am brilliant—otherwise be a big phony!" There are three types of agents:

1. Sneaky liar shits.
2. Busy, say-what-you-want-to-hear, okay-intentioned money-mongers.
3. Not-so-bads.

Pick whichever is right for you!

The Money Lover's Guide to Making Money

> "Banks are like magicians, hiding your money
> in their hand and pulling it out from behind
> your ear, but then putting it in their pocket
> as if you didn't see."
>
> —Eugene Mirman, from his off-Broadway musical
> *The Magic of Banking*

The wealthy, the impoverished, capitalists, communists, fat people, and drug lords agree: Money is important. It fuels modern civilization. Even before conventional paper notes and silver coins, ancient people tried to become affluent by owning and trading live, edible money—cattle, goats, even bears (not really—no one raised bears).

Ever since humanity moved from a simple bartering system to a monetary one (thanks, ancient Lydia or possibly China), people have fought hard not only to have enough to feed themselves and their families, but to have an abundance—to become tycoons, oligarchs, or upper-middle-class homeowners.

Technology and time have changed the landscape of finance.

Three thousand years ago, no one could have dreamed of auto manufacturing plants, online banks (not even the wise King Solomon), or the amazing cow-shrinking bags today's farmers use to transport cattle to pay bills with. It would have seemed impossible!

This modern landscape requires a new kind of financial citizen. Everyone is capable of willing themselves economic riches (except for those in extremely disenfranchised countries—which is most people, but probably not you!—and, of course, the genuinely mentally retarded—again, probably not you). If you like, once you become rich, you can build a machine that empowers poor, foreign, mentally injured peoples, but for now you must put these inequities aside. It's time to make money and grow that money into power, security, good deeds, high self-esteem (if you're lucky), or undeserved arrogance (if you're a dick).

Banking

Hope you're prepared, because I report your answers back to FEMA and they make their policies based on your answers to my pop quiz about banking (which is why I take some of the responsibility for their lack of readiness during Hurricane Katrina).

   1.   To make a lot of money from a bank you should:
       a. Open one account and put a lot of money in it.
       b. Open several accounts under different names.   ▶

c. *Open an overseas account and hide stolen money in it.*

d. *Go in guns-a-blazing and rob it.*

e. *This question is misguided!*

2. Who is the person at the bank you need to impress the most?

a. *The bank manager.*

b. *The "inside man."*

c. *The bank's daughter.*

d. *No one. This is a business, not an Impress-a-thon.*

3. When you look straight into a security camera, which phrase should you seductively mouth?

a. *"I want to fuck you."*

b. *"What's up?"*

c. *"I want to start a go-cart racing league."*

d. *"My ass is a playground, and it's recess, motherfucker."*

4. What is the number one mistake in banking?

a. *Not watching out for crazy, unreasonable fees.*

b. *Showing up drunk and trying to open an account with a piece of ribbon.*

c. *Making cat sounds to the teller.*

d. *Talking to an ATM as if it were in the future.*

Mortgages/Loans

Most places want to lend you money and want you to pay it back as slowly as possible so that they eventually get all your money. You

> *"Babies know."*
>
> —Eugene Mirman, from his book *The Innocence of Investment*

should totally borrow money from them, but then also secretly take something of theirs that they value more than money—like a childhood toy or spouse. You can pay people back at your own rate if you have their spouse.

Investment

Your question: What types of investments are out there? Good question, douche bag. (Sorry.) There are all sorts of investments available: stocks, bonds, mutual funds, commodities, options, David Bowie, and probably more. You'd have to ask an expert—not someone claiming to be an expert.

Warning: It is still risky to listen to an expert, because he might not admit he is part charlatan. (I use "he" not because of grammatical conventions, but because ladies would never misrepresent themselves regarding your finances.)

So what should you do? I don't think you should invest in commodities (gold, coffee, corn, etc.). Eddie Murphy made it seem risky in *Trading Places* (and the financial advice in *The Golden Child* is completely untrustworthy).

I know you. Here's your situation: You are sitting at home staring at a check for ten thousand dollars in a shoebox. (Why did you put your check in a shoebox?) You'd like to turn that check into a nice but modest house on Martha's Vineyard. Here's the secret that so many high-level traders use: Ask a nine-year-old, a thirteen-year-old, and a nineteen-year-old what new technology they are into. Then put a bunch of money in those technologies. And obviously, don't forget to diversify. (If you're racist, don't worry; "diversify" means something different in terms of money. No one is asking you to accept people for who they are and the sum of their thoughts and actions.)

> *"If God gave you a credit card, is that what you'd buy?"*
> —Eugene Mirman, from his undelivered 2004 commencement
> speech for Ithaca College, entitled "Rhetorical Questions"

Credit/Debt

They are making it harder to run up a lot of debt and then declare bankruptcy, but I'm sure you'll find a way to trick them. Be careful, credit is very addictive (somewhere between heroin and Pringles).

Try to pay debt off as soon as you can, or simply go off the grid and disappear for ten years. (No contacting anyone!) Once you return to civilization, there will be a big party, you can make up a story about being lost in a forest, and no creditor would risk coming after you for obvious PR reasons.

Venture Capital

Are you one of the many people with tens of millions of dollars who are unsure how to turn it into hundreds of millions of dollars? You're not alone. Did you know that about .00001 percent of the earth's population also shares that problem? I know. You're tired of starting charities and buying houses, planes, and fast things. You want to make something special. Like any kind of investing, it's important to diversify. However, I offer a unique plan: divide what you'd like to invest in half. Then invest one half in some sort of genius-sounding new technology or medicine. The second half, you should give to me. I will then divide that money in half and return half to you two years later and keep the rest. Shhhhhhh. No questions. Go.

Retirement Plan

Dig a trench one hundred feet deep. Each day put twenty-five dollars in it. I'm sure if you tell your employer what you're doing they will want to match it because of what a fun idea it is. At the end of forty years, you'll have upwards of seven hundred thousand dollars. Not bad. Plus, this way, if the economy collapses, you will have a pit full of money!

Politics

The Theory and Practice of
Organizations Connected with Government, I Think

The Origin of Politics

Politics is a delicious poison—an acrid nectar—it's a dirty luxury that the rich wear to hide the falseness behind their smiles. Not! Fooled you into thinking some eighteenth-century jackass took control of me!

Back in the late 1950s, I ran a small but influential political consulting firm in downtown Boston called Wicked Awesome Consultants (jokingly called WAC by my contemporaries). A young senator came to me one Tuesday afternoon and said, "I want to be the next president of the United States." I looked at him, made him get into a sensory deprivation tank and answer a few deceptively simple questions, and after about an hour, I said, "Okay, kid, let's do this." That person, of course, was John F. Kennedy, the thirty-fifth president. So do with my advice as you will, but keep in mind that I've worked in the shadows of thousands of campaigns for centuries (and brought down Joseph McCarthy, poisoned Stalin, and coined the term "muckraker").

So what is politics? Politics is simply how groups of people in various countries run their governments. Some countries (that are assholes—China, Uzbekistan, Utah—LOL!) run their countries like a prison, while others run their countries like a pretend not-prison—i.e., citizens believe they are free and they don't want leave, but also, they can't. (Keep in mind that I am only trying to make an Almost Point.) The best examples of this are Russia and *Star Trek*'s various idealized-worlds-with-a-dark-secret, but I bet there are other places. I will give you the gift of allowing you to come up with your own examples and discussing them with someone whose respect you badly desire. You're welcome. (I should have called this book *A Thousand Mind-Gifts*! Ha!)

The origin of politics can be traced back to the ancient city of Troy in 5000 BBJ (Before Billy Joel—religion and modern American culture clashed in 1980 with Billy Joel's first number one hit, "It's Still Rock and Roll to Me," and most modern cultural anthropologists of the savvy Generation C regard Billy Joel's artistic birth as a cultural rebirth—which is very verbose for something we both know is untrue).

History has witnessed endless ways that people have tried to rule themselves and rule others—feudalism, democracy, dictatorships, communism, socialism, libertarianism (never really tried), and anarchy (not the form that punk rockers would claim, but more like small self-governing communities).

HISTORY OF POLITICS

3000 B.C.E. Troy is founded.

Caesar is assassinated. **March 15, 44 B.C.E**

1914 – 1918 WWI

American Revolution, first time people vote on horseback. **1776**

March 4, 1797 George Washington givesup power, which is fucking cool of him to do.

Soviet Union is formed. Lenin issues all citizens mustache and goatee. Those who do not wear it are imprisoned. First sign that communism is iffy. **1922**

1933 First "New Deal" enacted by FDR mostly to scare Ronald Reagan.

FDR secretly builds an underground orgy room (which he nicknames the "Love Bunker") to get mind off of the Great Depression. **1935**

1936 Stalin starts killing everyone with whom he comes in contact.

Hitler is *Time* magazine's Man of the Year. **1938**

1939 – 1945 Hitler declares himself "World's Greatest Asshole." (In German, "Größtes Arschloch Der Welt.")

C.I.A formed. Jason Bourne trilogy becomes a semi-plausible storyline. **1947**

1948 Israel is formed. Ha ha, Hitler.

McCarthyism. People are put on **1950 something or so**
orly filmed black and white trials for having intellectual friends.

Iran is terrible. **1979**

1960 Students for a Democratic Society is founded, to the delight of Phil Ochs.

1980 Robert Ludlum's book *The Bourne Identity* is published.

s N' Roses releases "Welcome to yhe Jungle", a song about the dirty debauchery of L.A. rock 'n' roll. **1987**

1988 GN'R releases the controversial song "One in a Million", which the media ridiculed as homophobic and racist, while Axl Rose insisted the song "shined a brutal light on the racial and prejudicial ills in our society." (That isn't an actual quote, I just used quotation marks to illustrate that he said something to that effect).

Berlin Wall falls because Reagan yelled at it. **1989**

1992 Disregarding GN'R's various musical warnings, George Bush Sr. does nothing to prevent the L.A. riots.

North American Free Trade Agreement **1994**
goes into effect resulting in the acquittal of Lorena Bobbitt by reason of mental insanity.

1998 Bill Clinton engages a Code 5 Sex War on democracy.

Super-Republicans ruin America. **1999**

2000 The Cheney Doctrine limits the amount of fun is allowed in the world.

Uh oh. **2001**

2002 George W. Bush's foreign policy forces many Arabs to yell on television.

Putin launches Operation Sneaky-Jerk-Face. **2005**

2006 Danish cartoons infuriate radical Islamists; Kim Jong-il broadcasts the sound of his dick slapping a watermelon on short wave radio, hoping to get attention. It works.

The Great "Space Lie." Poor people are put into rocket ships that are never launched. **2007**

2008 Change change change change change change change change.

Change change change change change change change? **2010**

2012 Canada gives up.

What Do You Believe?

There is an endless supply of political theories and it isn't easy to decide which one is best for the economy, national security, education and health care, and which one will prevent teens from having sex (except oral, right?). Each of them has good ideas, and even more of them have terrible ideas but very good intentions. "The road to hell is paved with good intentions" is a pretty famous saying because of how true it is, *not* because it is a Randy Travis lyric. In fact, friend, most popular quotations are famous because of how true they are, with the exception of "Yippee ki yay, motherfucker!"

Here's a graph looking at a political spectrum, showing some of the different kinds of governments that exist in the world.

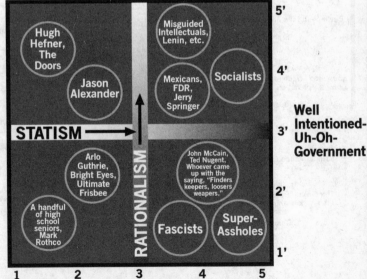

Here is a chart of attitudes toward a variety of social issues that are a part of America's on going culture wars. (TV show idea alert! *Culture Wars*—about a group of conflicted abortion doctors who try to ban same-sex marriage!)

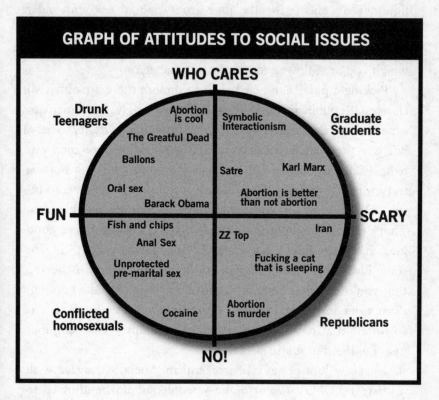

GRAPH OF ATTITUDES TO SOCIAL ISSUES

WHO CARES

Drunk Teenagers

Abortion is cool

The Greatful Dead

Ballons

Oral sex

Barack Obama

Symbolic Interactionism

Satre   Karl Marx

Abortion is better than not abortion

Graduate Students

FUN

Fish and chips

Anal Sex

Unprotected pre-marital sex

ZZ Top

Iran

Fucking a cat that is sleeping

SCARY

Conflicted homosexuals

Cocaine

Abortion is murder

Republicans

NO!

"America is a melting pot, but some cultures are accidentally burned."

—Eugene Mirman, joking around with Noam Chomsky at Sherman Café in Union Square, Somerville

Political Parties in America
....

In American culture, when you are eighteen you ascend to warrior class—you are allowed to drive, join the Army, sneak liquor into a movie theater, joke around about sex with older people at a park, and most importantly: you must choose a political party to vote for and belong to for five to ten years (after which you are allowed to revisit the issue again).

Picking a party can be hard, even though there are only two choices: Republican or Democrat. Interestingly, an American supermarket would overwhelm some foreigners with its variety, but our political parties would not (unless the foreigner was from Fear-and-murder-istan). Idealistic youths may go outside traditional boundaries and choose communism or libertarianism. This is okay, except communism, which is a terrible idea. That's right—I don't even think idealized communism is a good idea. It's state-sanctioned slavery! Zing, Karl Marx! (Still, for some idealists, one of the perks of being in college is believing that you're the first person to figure out how to make communism work in the real world.) I know, in some countries life is so unfair that it would be better if the country were communist. I agree. But it still sucks.

I get the lure of sexy libertarianism. Socially, I agree with a libertarian POV (Point of V)—people should be allowed to amass great wealth, fuck chickens (dead, of course), have a gun, and suck on each other's wingy-dings—but we also need education, police, health care, some arts, libraries, etc. Otherwise, all the poor people will get so down and out that they'll eat all the rich people (*read: Jews*), and I don't want that to happen in America. Politics is about placating people so that they don't revolt and eat you. And what better placation than actually providing shelter, education, protection, and health care? Nothing, really.

Now that you don't want to be a communist or libertarian, what can you be? There are two choices: Democrat, Republican, and Independent. (I added a third to appease you.) Don't get me wrong—if you'd like to belong to one of the well-meaning fringe parties, you can. It will give people at get-togethers someone to point and scowl at.

I'll go over the three main groups to help you choose which one you'll belong to.

Democrats

Pro: Democrats want things to be fair for everyone, even those that are lazy. They want to save the environment, have great schools, promote racial and sexual equality, keep abortion legal, hold midnight sex parties, legalize staying up late and talking about pot, embezzling, etc. They are loose, sexually irresponsible, and often high (all of which feels great!). They want peace, unless there are civilians getting shot in public squares, then they get pretty gung ho about a quick war.

Con: Democrats can be smug, condescending, and hypocritical in a super annoying way. Most democrats would not actually wash a Hispanic person if someone asked them to. (This is a bad example, because most people wouldn't wash any stranger.) Another problem is that historically there is a lot of corruption. In Boston, corrupt democrats did lots of crappy things, and that's their home base. In New York in the late 1800s and early 1900s, the Tammany Hall machine was a no-good-son-of-a-bitch. Luckily, it was dismantled by FDR, the Sub-Mariner and Iron Man.

Republicans

Pro: Republicans respect hard work, making money, and keeping the money you make. They love a nuclear family and traditional (i.e., *lame*) values (unlike Democrats, who are working on a secret Divorce Ray; they have already perfected a ray that turns 10 percent of the population gay and another that is increasing the number of minorities inside *and* outside of the U.S.). Republicans enjoy a strong army and are suspicious of mustachioed foreigners (as they should be). Republicans are also the only ones who remember 9/11. (Whatever that was, right?)

Con: Some Republicans (no thanks to the 1980s!) want to bring about the end of the world. Also, they tend to have same-sex affairs (which they hate in theory—but *love* in practice), making them hypocritical about the one area of the body they want to pass laws against.

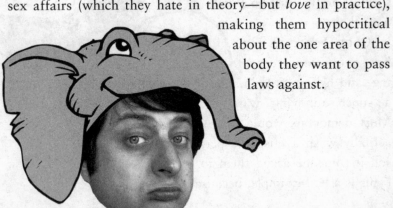

Independents

Pro: You get to pick whatever you like from the political spectrum and claim it as your own. You are smart and special and not constrained by partisanship or dogma. During the primaries, people care what you think.

Con: You will never have an electable leader you can totally get behind (other than Ross "I'm Goofy" Perot and Ralph "Not as Good as I Seem" Nader), and many of your compatriots are wrestlers and kooks.

Answer the Following Questions to Figure Out Your Political Party

There can be a lot of noise out there, so I've come up with some questions for you to answer to help you figure out which party is right for you:

1. I hate taxes, because I work hard for my money, but:
   a. *No, that's it. I hate taxes.*
   b. *We need schools and police.*
   c. *I want to walk around with a sword.*

2. I am afraid of foreigners trying to blow us up:
   a. *I don't care if they tap my phones. I'm not doing anything wrong.*
   b. *I have phone sex a lot, so I'd rather the feds didn't know that I make voice-hookers pretend to shit in my mouth.*
   c. *Thomas Jefferson said, "The strongest reason for the people to retain the right to keep and bear arms is, as a last resort, to protect themselves against tyranny in government." I say it in my sleep.*

3. Same sex marriage is:
   a. *A gateway into a dangerous world where everyone is gay and horses run the government.*
   b. *The most fun you can have on a Wednesday.*
   c. *I don't care! I just want to play dress-up in my compound!*

4. If someone attacks us:
   a. *We should wipe them off the face of the earth, even if it means self-destruction.*
   b. *Write them an angry letter explaining why we're upset.*
   c. *Go off the grid; bring canned food, weapons, and a lover.*

If you answered A to three or more, then you'd probably feel most comfortable as a Republican. If you answered B to most, then you're a Democrat. If you said C to all of them, you're a bit of a kook. However, if you threw in one or two Cs, you're probably just thoughtful, independent, and slightly paranoid. Congratulations! Now you have a party to belong to, and it comes with a whole lot of perks—friends, potential mates, business associates—and a lot of opinions to vigorously debate at Belle and Sebastian meet-ups.

Protests: From Getting &@#! Done, to Fucking &@#! Up, to Fucking the Shit Out of So#Eone

As everyone knows, corporations meet with the government every January 25 to decide what lies they will sell the public that year. Though this is common knowledge, only a handful of citizens ever do anything about it. I call those citizens The Dalai Lama, which I know is someone else, but I don't care and it's a free country—or is it?

Some people who go to protests just want a place to express their individuality, while others are responsible citizens who want to make a difference, and yet a third group are simply horny, emotional, and often disoriented. It doesn't really matter what your reason for showing up is, as long as the event *looks* impressive.

There is nothing sadder than walking past five passionate people in their late fifties and early sixties (maybe with a few twenty-somethings) in Ann Arbor, Michigan, (or a similar place) who have a few homemade signs that say STOP THE WAR or COME ON, MAN! STOP THE WAR, OKAY? Nothing tells the government to keep doing what they're doing like a small number of seemingly confused protesters defeated on a street corner. Do not hold a tiny protest, please. Hold only big ones. That means 150 people or more. No one person can meet 150 people and remember them in a day, and a group of 150 people looks like a lot. Okay? Good.

If you sort of care about the protest, but mostly are there to meet like-minded lovers, then be on your best behavior. Wear a nice outfit that's casual enough to be at a protest, but sexy and suave enough to attract a life-partner. Try to be up on the details of whatever you're protesting. Nothing is *less* sexy than if someone is commenting on the atrocities at Abu Ghraib and you respond by asking whether Abu Ghraib is a band that *sucks*.

If you have it in your heart, don't wear some sort of crazy Dr. Seuss jester hat or wacky outfit. I know it seems fun, but you'll end up on television and it will look like only clowns and various children's entertainers are worried about global warming. Think of it this way: Al Gore has done a lot to help the environment, and how much less effective would he have been if he'd worn a two-foot-tall multicolored felt hat? I know, it's not fair that people are so superficial, but until society matures, you're going to have to hold some of your creativity inside. I'm sorry.

How to Talk to an Arrogant, Radical College Student
....

Here's the thing: Sometimes inspired college kids (and college-age kids) have a passion and force of will that can create real, positive change. They are often the cultural catalyst that is needed to end a crappy war or bring about civil equality. (I'm sure that they will be at the forefront of helping self-aware robots vote.) However, it can be annoying when a person falls short of enacting change and is mostly motivated by guilt about his fancy upbringing. Just like an injured wolf, an embarrassed congressman, or a teenager that is so mad at her parents she is willing to do things in a high school bathroom that should normally only be done by consensual adults at exclusive parties, these often confused and injured young people are capable of doing or saying almost anything to survive and find their way.

I went to Hampshire College, a very liberal arts school. There were generally two kinds of activists: the impassioned and effective; and the weird, lonely, and loud. At Hampshire, many were both. Our college's library steps were littered with Maoists from New Jersey taking responsibility for Stalin's excessive executions. (I still don't understand what it means for an American teenager to take responsibility seventy years later for the atrocities of the former Soviet Union, but I'd love to put them on trial in front of a world court.) There were constant protests and demonstrations (with varying degrees of validity). Once, some folks tried to set the lawn free by placing large rocks all over campus so that it couldn't be mowed. Those people were retarded and on heroin. Another time, kids painted the wall of our student center white, called it the Democracy Wall, and protested when it had to be washed away. "How will our voices be heard?" they cried, as the painted bathroom-stall political slogans were blasted away with high-powered water hoses. (The answer was that their voices could be heard the way you hear voices—by their organizing demonstrations and meetings, creating organizations, writing letters, circulating petitions, and whatever other means mostly privileged upper-middle-class white teens have at their disposal—which now includes podcasts.)

One of my favorite demonstrations was held during my first week there. It was a rally demanding chicken rights. Real people spoke not about preventing animal cruelty (or even animal consumption), but about chickens' inalienable rights. Nobody likes it when a farmer punches a chicken (though punched chickens taste the best), but to insist that chickens have the right to avoid self-incrimination in court? That's too much, Mr. Hippie. Plus, drug-dealing chickens shouldn't have an easy out—they fucked up; they do the time. If some chicken molests a little boy (even a bully), you're telling me it should have a fair trial? Fuck that. Prison, Mr. Chicken.

At the time I attended university, there was no war (that anyone knew of—right, CIA?). We didn't have the good fortune of an unpopular war to rally against to help us make friends in this new, scary (and promiscuous!!!!!) environment. So, many of us had to pick a cause and fight for what we loved, which was often marijuana (the result of letting a black light and Pink Floyd poster determine your politics).

Hey, everybody wants pot to be legalized, right? It is sort of basically legal (unless you're a dealer—be careful). Nobody really cares about it except a few feds and mothers who mistakenly think it's a gateway drug. (The only way pot is a gateway drug is that it takes some people to another dimension—where it is okay to just eat chips and burritos and watch children's television.) Marijuana even has countless medical purposes. (Psychologists have used pot on OCD patients to make their organs tingle so that they don't cry and freak out during copulation.) When a bearded nineteen-year-old guy in a skirt pickets in the center of a small college town, yelling at old people, elementary school teachers, and councilmen about how pot could be used to make parachutes, rope, and save lives, it can be a turnoff, especially if he's spitting when he talks.

These people come in and out of our lives enough that it's important to try to get along with them. Many of the causes they support are good and just; it's just (both uses of the word "just" alert!) that their method grates against the fabric of pleasing social interaction. Here are a few things you can do and say to engage and relax an arrogant and stinky college student:

1. Use your voice as a weapon, like you do when you disarm an attacker in a parking garage and get right in their face and yell, "I completely agree, but you need to be quieter!" Then kick them in the groin.

2. Bring them a quiche and tell them it's a gift from a monk and they must eat it right away. Make the quiche with valerian root, so they become sleepy.
3. Douse them in water, hug them, and whisper, "I love you."

Sadly, those are the only three things that you can do. Maybe as things change and people evolve, there will be better ways to engage each other in an open dialogue about the future of mankind. But for now, there isn't a good way to talk to someone who is covered in fake blood, shaking their head, and pointing at you in a disapproving way.

Starting a New Political Movement
....

Starting a new political movement is simple, but getting people involved in it is tough. Plan out your ideal political system, and then create a series of rewards as incentive for people to join your cause (which can be anything from political change to cash or a live monkey). Keep the following things in mind:

1. Everybody loves to be part of a community.
2. People like to talk about something as if they know what they are talking about. So give them lots of facts to assert, accurate or not.
3. Israel and Palestine are mad at each other.
4. It is easier to get people politically involved if they think they might fall in love or make friends.
5. Children are people until the age of fourteen.
6. Don't let how terrible things are in some parts of the

world make you snap, so that instead of enacting change, you yell at food service people. It won't make you a good leader.

You've pretty much got all the tools you need. Just find a meeting place, some like-minded folks, and get ready to make a difference. One secret to starting a political movement is making your top priorities the same as other people's—the economy, national security, education, the environment, etc.— but throw in a few oddball ones that people can also really get behind. Like what?

1. Technology is threatening to destroy the earth and we need to get rid of anything that doesn't involve cooking or transportation. (Always include a flaw to help foster arguments with strangers.)
2. We need to remove all the salt from the world's oceans by 2020. (*Never* reveal why.)
3. The number one priority is for America to construct another New York City on the moon. Or at *least* a Providence, Rhode Island.
4. To protect America's sovereignty, we must build a clone army out of Matt Damon.
5. Everyone on the planet should be issued a Hugh Hefner mask so that when aliens attack, they won't be able to tell who the leader is. The aliens will then have an emotional breakdown and leave.

Celebrities and Politics
••••••••••••••••••••••••••••••••

Celebrities like to help out. Many of them feel guilty (especially actors) for being so admired for their attractiveness or Pretendings. (That's what entertainment industry insiders call acting.) Some impassioned celebrities get really involved in politics and activism, like Bono, Angelina Jolie, Paul Newman, Ted Nugent, and even former actor Ronald Reagan (who seems to be the only Republican celebrity anyone can recall). Pamela Anderson is a member of PETA (even though her giant tits aren't! There! I said what you were thinking!).

You may find it annoying that celebrities tell you what they think about government and social issues, but honestly, that's your punishment for following their relationships in the news and masturbating to the sound of their lives falling apart. As a result, you have to listen to the political musings of Chuck Norris, or if you're more fortunate, those of George Clooney.

What I can offer you are some stress-reducing exercises to relax in case a celebrity endorses something you hate because you're a jerk, because they're super preachy, or because what they are saying is truly, fundamentally, idiotic. There are two techniques that I use myself:

1. Order Chinese food, get a few bottles of wine, run a warm bath, and invite friends over for an impromptu Bathroom Party.
2. Go to a wooded area and bring acrylic paints and a canvas. Put on your favorite mix of mellow tunes. Gulp down about four Advil PMs, a beer, a bottle of port, a vase full of Grey Goose vodka, a pint of crème de cacao; eat a box of pot; make fancy mac and cheese; and unwind

(and start painting). The next day, call Sotheby's and let them know you have some paintings that are worth millions. After you sell them, you will be famous enough to start the cycle again, but this time, as the celebrity! That's how I did it. See?

I Am a Celebrity and I'd Like to Get Involved

First, a warning: Do people perceive you to be on the far left or far right? Then be careful—if it's a cause you're fighting for (like ending homelessness or getting the word out to teenagers that they have to be good looking to succeed), you'll probably help; but if it's a candidate, you may hurt them, because average people might think you're crazy. Which you're probably not, *buuuuut*—you might be crazy (either because of drugs or a heavy metal accident, or because you've spent the past six years reading about mind-boggling global injustice, and you snapped—so you *want* to help the world, but instead, you cry every time you make a sandwich).

But you know what? Fuck it. And fuck all the naysayers. It's time to get up and make a difference. So put on your balls (regardless of gender), eat a thousand gumption-filled Hot Pockets, get a clipboard, a video camera, a photograph of a poor child riding a fucked up lab animal (to constantly remind you how sick this world is), and get out there and start helping. Make sure to wear something sexy, because remember: you are talking to sheep—and sheep love nice jeans hugging cute buns, both ladies' and gentlemen's.

As a celebrity, you can make more of an impact than others (except members of Foreigner—sorry, your popularity is inversely proportionate to your influence). However, generally, the people who will be most affected by your opinion are teens and tweens, who are powerless (except for their buying dollar!!!!!). It's a truth we all have to accept. I probably stopped listening to Mr. T's advice when I turned seventeen (definitely by the age of twenty-two).

Here are some potential ways to support various causes and have an impact as a celebrity:

1. Farmers being exploited. There is already a good support system in place. Just text FARMERS IN DANGER to Rage Against the Machine's Tom Morello. He'll do the rest. (Although this doesn't seem like much, as a celebrity it's your job to text other celebrities with actionable information.)

2. Animal rights and fur. As an Animal Rights Celebrity (ARC) you must pose naked—with a raccoon!—for a photograph with the caption OUR FUR, NOT YOURS! You can also organize discussions in which you educate eccentrics and rappers about the unsavory process of fur production. (Make sure you do not direct your message at people in countries where fur is necessary for trade and warmth; you'll be branded as xenophobic—JK—in cold climates, people are already xenophobic and racist themselves! JK again! Just the Ukraine.)

3. World hunger. The great thing about this one is that

everyone wants to end it. Only some very fringe people be-lieve hunger is necessary for thinning the world population or something. So that's great. Example: Pretty much everybody admires Bobo (I mean Bono, sorry) for what he's done to fight poverty and world hunger. There are three main ways of fight-ing world hunger: money, awareness, and food. Figure out which one you would like to raise and get moving. Some quick fixes:

a. *Donate all your money to a helpful organization (like UNICEF or AFTRA).*

b. *Organize a global game of telephone (using actual tele-phones) where you call ordinary people (who you'll ask to call ten people) and tell them to stop being numb to the world and to "Wake the Fuck Up." (I put it in quotes because that's what you should call the event. If you want to make it sound more official, you can add "America" to the end.) It will be awesome to see what the message is when it comes back to you through some of the very people you're trying to help.*

4. The environment. Other than a handful of crazy su-perconservatives and frustrated Chinese bureaucrats, everyone believes it's time to help save the earth. This little blue marble is all you have (I can leave at any time), so it's up to everyone to take care of it. As a celebrity, you are in a unique position to motivate people by singing a song about it. Make it available as a free download. What should the lyrics be? That's up to you, but here's a verse to start you off:

> *Hey, Mother Earth, I want to fly to Paraguay*
> *To play in their sand and maybe poison their land*

Can't you understand . . . it's to create jobs, not to robs . . .
  you, Mama
Hey, Mr. Human, go ahead and play, but you're making me
  pay (by dying)
For your greedy mistakes, like you won't have steaks (in a
  hundred years)
Rivers run with tears . . . of acid rain
Earth wastes away something something pain pain. . .
All over our planet people born without tits
Southern children eating hair instead of grits
Dead trees and hookers fill the streets and everything is on
  fire. . .
Fuck, Mama, I'm so sorry. . .

"The more you know, the more you know, right?"

—Eugene Mirman, asking his cat a rhetorical question

World Governments from Around the World

Although America's brand of democracy is top notch, there are other ways to run a country, all types of governments, with their assorted laws and varying applications of free market to command economies. (I think I'm right, but I don't really know what I'm talking about.) To explain how to effectively participate or borrow from (or run!!!) all these different kinds of governments, I could fill a fifty-thousand-page document unwisely titled *Hey, Buddy! World Government from A to Shoes*. But that's for another time, friend (hopefully not, actually). Soon, we have to get to death and the afterlife; we can't spend our time tinkering with the ins and outs of Swedish capitalism or hostile dictatorships and their associates. Or can we? Well, maybe a little. . .

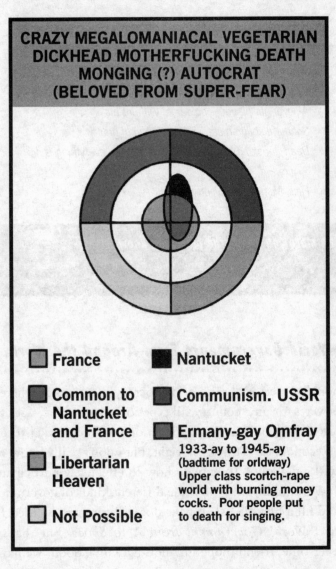

Socialism or So-So-Ism: Which Is It, Europe?

From the hundreds of weekly letters I get from people in all walks of life (though to be honest, most are from Charles Bronson), many Europeans (and some Israelis) are always asking me how they can milk their nations' generosity for their selfish gain. To be fair, I get an equal number of letters from regular Americans (like you) asking how they can help their local government apply some of Europe's savvy socialist elements to their system.

History tells us Europe has been around for *more than twice* as long as America, yet the nations of Europe have tried to conquer each other so many times it's left them weak, and now, we are their masters. (Don't worry, they can't see this; they are too busy trying on crazy, multicolored sweaters and sleek, zipper-covered pants.)

Still, excluding their crippling taxes, limitations on free speech, gun-o-phobia (reasonable), deep anti-Semitism (also reasonable), general rudeness, and occasional inability to express emotion (except in France and Portugal), some things Europeans have done well is figure out how to be generally affluent, vacation more, provide everyone with health care, and have great schools. I'm not sure if they put much money into their armies anymore, but that's okay, because we all remember what happened last time, right? Whether you live in a socialist country and want to get your (and others) fair share, or simply want to incorporate some of their inventiveness into your life, like anything, there are a few easy things you can do.

If You Live in a Slightly Socialist Country and Would Like to Take Advantage of Their Generosity:

1. Fake your own death and collect your Death Reward instead of your family. (To decrease health care costs, most European countries offer incentives for people to help their elderly relatives have unexpected "accidents.")
2. Go to the hospital and tell them you need pain killers. Sell those pain killers to traveling Americans. You just made five hundred euros!
3. Call in sick every day for eight years.
4. Write a letter to your prime minister requesting fifty thousand euros for "a really cool rave that will lift the nation's spirits." Most European constitutions have a law that disallows them from turning down an offer to hold a rave.

If You Live in America (or a Barely Socialist Country) and Would Like to Apply a Tad of Socialist Ingenuity to Your Town:

1. Start a weekly art film night in your community to raise money for schools, but actually put the money into an offshore account that you use to improve the lives of prostitutes—*your* prostitutes!
2. Go to a different emergency room each morning under a different name and see what medicine you can collect.
3. Move to Nevada and don't gamble.
4. Start a movement where rude waiters provide people with small amounts of great food over a long time. Call it a "French restaurant." On the bill, have them add a made-up 7 percent tax called the Fuck You American Tax.

Quick Tips for Running a Communist Empire

Communism relies heavily on the "grass is always greener" argument. When a country is at the edge of economic ruin because of Cheneyesque free-market brouhaha, it becomes weak. Communism is like a mortgage scam, preying upon the downtrodden. (I know, unfettered capitalism is a cruel monkey as well.) I guess, ultimately, everyone loves power and wealth, and the nature of many people (especially the Japanese businessmen who exploit women in movies and in at least one episode of *Law and Order*) is an unempathetic callousness to human suffering. It does at least provide us with our villains.

If you find yourself at the head of a communist government, here's some ways to stay there . . .

Top Tips for Communist Countries (Warning: These Are Mostly Zings)

1. First of all, don't forget to use fear as a control tactic.
2. Always talk like a sexual predator who claims what he's doing is best for the victim.
3. Never smile. It betrays your authority. (In most communist countries, smiling is considered submissive and something that only prostitutes and school children do.)
4. Never, ever swear.
5. Do not report any kind of bad news. It will lead to revolution.
6. If someone gives you trouble, lean on their parents' business so they stop. Never kill too many people who are close to a troublemaker. He'll become too powerful, like Luke Skywalker or Daredevil. And the last thing your communist regime needs is a superhuman costumed hero out for vengeance.

Autocracy: Becoming One of Two Kinds of Dictators

There are two basic kinds of dictators: the well-meaning dictator who is somewhat brutal, and the not-even-pretending-to-not-kill-his-own-people dictator. The first could be anything from a dictator who truly wants to help his people, to a guy who has a personal get-rich-quick scheme (Putin!), to both (Puts again). They are your general peasant king, sneaky prime minister, or emperor, like Caesar, Napoleon, the aforementioned Putinator, King George, etc. Some dictators just love power. Some love money. Some love their countries. Most love all three.

The second kind of dictator—the kind who enjoys pointing at someone in the street and having them brought to his weird sex room (Saddam)—has gone by many names: Saddam Hussein, Pol Pot, Joey Stalins, and probably others, but why would you need more than three examples? Fine. Here are some more: Adolf Hitler, Czar Nicholas II, Yahya Khan (not to be confused with Khan Noonien Singh from *Star Trek II: The Wrath of Khan*; though also vicious, the latter Khan is fictional).

Each of these people has found ways to seize power, hold on to that power, and make unilateral decisions for their nations (not to mention the great food and unlimited pussy at their fingertips—pretty cool, right, bro?). Some use force, some use propaganda, but all pride themselves on having absolute power and a sweet cult of personality. Want to seize your nation by the throat and fix it? You can, if you're clever. Either way, these are some things to keep in mind throughout your initial take-over and following rule.

Tips for Dictators

Regardless of what kind of dictator you want to be, you're going to have to do the same sort of things to varying degrees. (Just change up the language you use depending on the results you want.)

1. Make roots in the intelligence community. Information is power. So are secret ways to assassinate and torture people.
2. Take evening classes in charisma and megalomania. It is vital to develop a God complex.
3. Find a scapegoat. Jews are obviously good, but try to look outside the traditional scapegoat communities for new scapegoats. It will throw people off (foreign and domestic) and be easier in this new global community, with savvier citizenry. Maybe try old people in moterized wheelchairs?
4. Eat right. A healthy dictator is a long-lasting dictator.
5. And of course: Don't forget to have a stranglehold on all the media outlets!
6. Make sure to pick a nation to hate (or pretend to hate) and blame for economic problems.
7. Watch amateur porn in the mornings to control your aggression levels.
8. Have a glass of mulled wine before going to sleep.

What Kind of Leader Are You?

Now that you know what kind of leadership styles exist all over the world, it's time to figure out what kind you'd be. Answer the following questions, and you'll know. Remember, no one cares how you answer these, so don't lie to yourself.

Take the Quiz

1. A national television channel has a talking head show that criticizes your leadership. You:
    a. *Kill everyone involved and their families.*
    b. *Kill everyone involved and issue a warning*
    c. *Shut down the TV station for "tax evasion" and take it over five months later under state control.*
    d. *Enjoy the healthy debate and simply issue harsher talking points the next morning (and maybe look into having some people slightly intimidated).*

2. A national weather-based tragedy of historic proportions devastates a poor region of your country. You:
    a. *Blame the United States and Israel for using an evil, capitalist weather machine to terrorize your nation.*
    b. *Respond quickly to the disaster through an organization that is not run by some guy who comes from Horse Leadership or something.*
    c. *Bomb the region to finish the job and then issue a statement saying that you in conjunction with God decided to eradicate these sinners.*
    d. *Text a bunch of old Navy buddies and tell them you need a hand and that there are free cupcakes in it for them.* ▶

3. A neighboring nation issues a statement saying that your country is a homosexual. You:
    a. *Fire back with your own homophobic disparagements.*
    b. *Agree with them and challenge them to a same-sex orgy (confusing, but more effective than you'd think).*
    c. *Use chemical weapons on them to deter further hate speech.*
    d. *Do not engage this question because it lacks substance and you are a real leader, with no time for fun. (This is a trick question, because if you have no time for fun, people will see you as stiff and mock you in bars.)*

4. Because of predatory lending, a botched war, rising unemployment, the collapse of your economy, a spike in organized crime, and the ban of religious artifacts in public, riots break out and your country's only hope for order is from a transvestite army. You:
    a. *Join them as their leader and restore your great state to its former glory.*
    b. *Abandon your failing nation and move to Italy, where you open a surprisingly successful bagel chain.*
    c. *Squelch the transvestites and infuse the country with money you stole.*
    d. *Do nothing and let the free hand of the market correct itself.*

That's the kind of leader you are! Now get to it! (Conquering.)

"The world is your oyster."

—Eugene Mirman, speaking to an oyster

The Ringing of Revolution

····································

The two rules of revolution are: Make sure over 65 percent of your country's population is being oppressed or in poverty before you start, and bring snacks. The two rules of staying in power after the revolution are similar: Do not jail or kill more than 35 percent of your population, and make sure there are enough snacks for 75 percent of the people.

These are, of course, just bare-bones estimates. To have a happy citizenry, you should consider not killing any percentage of your own people solely to stay in power, and not just because of some unspoken universal human morality, but mostly because it's gauche. (As a revolutionary, you can't admit how important social graces are to you, but we both know they are.)

It's done. The world is yours. You have the know-how, the skills, the tools, and the Will. There's only one realm you don't own, one place left to conquer (and I am not talking about the Christie Brinkley fun-zone or opening a Hardees franchise—two issues I purposely left out). It's time to take control, stop the second-guessing, and learn about death—and don't bring your preconceptions with you. Leave them here, please.

Death and the Afterlife

Goodtimes

For each of us, death, at least in this world, is a pretty likely outcome. Up till now, no one has lived forever (correction: no one who will admit it—right, John McCain's mom?). Eternal life in an afterlife is prized in almost every culture, but eternal life on earth is often portrayed as burdensome (because of all the problems we have—like dirty sidewalks, DVD bootlegging, traffic jams, etc.). Because of these earthly anguish-ies, it's okay that we'll die and move on to a better place. But where will we go, what should we bring, and how should we behave?

People think they want to live forever on earth, but really they

> ## *"I want to live forever!"*
> —Eugene Mirman, at a rest stop in Nevada, teasing a group of New Age potheads

just want to fly or have powers. Think about *Highlander* and that dictator who lives forever in the *Justice League* cartoon—it's a nuisance. Most eternal-life themed science fiction makes one thing clear: it is depressing and lonely to outlive all your friends every hundred years. Sure, living for eight hundred years can be great, like Yoda did. (If I am wrong about Yoda's age, consider not sending me an angry letter. Thanks, nerd!)

You're like, "What about the Holy Grail?" Fine, but that's more of an obsession with eternal youth, and stop bringing up things that divert me from my thesis. Regardless, it doesn't matter what fantasies people have, since the chances of your living longer than 110 years are *much* less than one in fifty. So let's stop focusing on the lofty goal of eternal life in this world, and focus on the very real goal of life in the next. That leaves us two questions: How should you die, and what happens once you do?

O Great Ways to Die

Along with losing your job, buying a house, divorce, and having a baby, dying is one of the most stressful things that can happen to you. Whatever you can do to ease the stress of death will greatly improve your life.

One good exercise is, instead of making a to-do list, make a "ways I don't want to die" list. Often, making your conscious mind aware of subconscious fears is a way to avoid them. Don't know where to begin? Here are some ideas for ways you may not want to die:

1. In a cave with a monster.
2. Horsing around on a helicopter.
3. PCP-induced cockiness.
4. Trying to break any kind of food-based record.

On the other hand, here are some great ways to die:

1. Peacefully, in your sleep.

2. While high-fiving.

3. Making love to a good friend.

4. Getting "zapped."

The Afterlife
· · · · · · · · · · · · · · · · · ·

Regardless of what your religion is, it's my job to prepare you for the afterlife. There are lots of rumors and speculation about the great beyond, but it's all conjecture, whatever conjecture is. Atheists believe that when you die, you'll just disappear. The belief is self-defeating, because it robs atheists of the opportunity to go to religious people, "I told you so." However, when the faithful die, they'll get to rub it in for a brief second as the damned pass before them into Damned-Land. I can only imagine the pleasure of being part of a chorus of billions of people getting to taunt a nonbeliever on their way to a Crappy Forever. (That's what I call every religion's concept of hell.)

> *"Don't worry, death is just a fresh start."*
> —Eugene Mirman, trying to comfort a child who badly hurt himself

Life After Death

The biggest misconception about the afterlife is that it's significantly different from regular life. It's not. Sure, you can't die again or be harmed physically, and there's no illness, cholesterol, or war. There is no money, but instead there is a complicated network of bartering (which is called Favor Swaps). However, many of the social dynamics that exist in our world exist in Heaven or "Goodtimes" (its actual interfaith name in the afterworld). For instance, dating is still awkward; so are loud dance clubs and some charity fundraisers.

Like any kind of intelligence-gathering, each of the major religions holds some truth, but each contains a lot of misinformation, inflated fears, and confusion. Here's a no-BS rundown about Goodtimes—what is actually accurate from each religion about the next life.

Christianity

You are greeted not just by your pets, but also the pets featured on hit television programs of the past fifty years. Also, you have access to unlimited seafood tapas and an enormous charcuterie plate.
It's actually pretty awesome. Plus, the Beatles run a bar where they play covers twenty-six hours a day.

Islam

Everyone is greeted by fifty-two virgins (not seventy-two) to party and sleep with. As much as men are comforted by the idea of having sex with a large number of inexperienced women, it is a cruel stroke of sexism that makes recently deceased Islamic women have sex with fifty-two inexperienced men. Without a doubt heaven has elements of a pretty crazy college party that never got videotaped and put online.

Judaism

Everyone is given lots of sweet wine and a newspaper to run.

I grant you dominion over radio and television once they exist. And don't forget — you can't eat lobsters or horses!

Buddhism

Food is plentiful and cheerful. That's right—everything that you eat thanks you when you eat it! It's really cool.

Atheism

There are clean, automated bathrooms.

Agnosticism

???????????????????????????????????? and ice cream.

All in all, Goodtimes is a pretty good place—with pets, good food, sex, a media outlet, and so much more. No wonder so many people are excited to get there, and no wonder most religions exclude suicide as a means—the line would be unbearable.

Things to Bring with You into the Next Life

You can bring anything you want into the afterlife with you, but some things are more useful than others. For instance, did you know that there is no granulated sugar? It's true. You may want to bring some if you bake a lot (though there are countless substitutes available: honey, corn syrup, molasses, brown sugar, etc.). Another odd fact: They have all the alcohol you want, but not that many mixers.

These staples may be hard to find:

1. Pornography (There is some soft-core, but not much.)
2. Bathing suit
3. Motorized vehicles (car, motorcycle, helicopter, boat, etc.)
4. Cranberry juice
5. Spatulas
6. Heavy metal and '70s hard rock. (They have tons of music, but most of it is '80s New Wave, '60s folk rock, early U2, modern hip-hop, and a lot of indie rock.)
7. Small foodstuff that can be used for magic and potions (beans, pumpkin seeds, nuts, dried fruit, etc.)
8. Fishing pole
9. Ink-jet cartridges and paper to print on
10. One nice suit or dress

How do you collect all these things? It's actually simple. The second you die, you're given a thousand magic stickers to put on things to take with you. The mistake that most people make is they put the stickers on all their sentimental belongings, but actually, these things will be there. A lot of ordinary items will not. Now you know—you're welcome.

Etiquette in Goodtimes

Manners are very important in the next life. The tricky part is that not all "good" manners are the same on both sides of the divide. For instance, the salad fork is for soup. It sounds counterintuitive because of the name of the object, but in Goodtimes, salad forks are actually magic spoons.

Different regions of Goodtimes have slightly different etiquette, so just ask around before you hold a door for someone the wrong way or don't throw up at the right time (generally, 5:30 p.m.). But the one rule to always remember: ?????????????????????. Sorry, but I have to keep *something* a secret about the next life, I promised a Big Old Bearded Guy (God!!!!!!!!!).

Badtimes

Is there such a place as "Badtimes" (i.e., Crappy Forever) for those who are wicked? No. Everyone wicked is turned into cheese and eaten. Sorry. In Goodtimes, the cheese is made from the damned. It's a fact. It's rarely discussed because people aren't as motivated to live a moral life when you say, "Hey, don't rape or rob a bank—or else in the next life you'll be made into cheese and eaten." It's not convincing, but the truth rarely is.

> *"In the end there is another beginning, making the end the beginning instead of the end . . . in a classic switcheroo."*
>
> —Eugene Mirman, trying to confuse a rabbi
> early one Sunday morning at an Indian buffet brunch

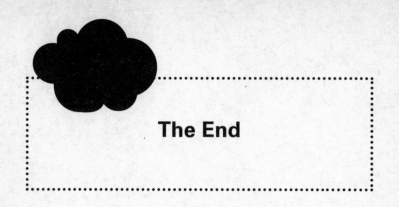

The End

First of all: Congratulations. You made it. You're wiser, stronger, and more *Willful-Tastic*. Second: You're welcome—you are now a Level 26 Human. I can only imagine the Über Mo-Fo you are now, with your long hair, solid-gold hat, and wonderful life-partner. If you've done even a franction (wait a second—there's no *n* in fraction!) of the nondangerous things I've suggested, you're probably a lot happier, own a small, weird business, and make love every two or three days. Even if you take only one small thing from this book and apply it to your life, I'll be able to say, "I empowered and/or tricked _____ ." (Fill in your name.)

I know that there is a lot missing from this book, and nothing is perfect. That doesn't mean that something can't be *perceived* as perfect. So as a favor to both of us, feel free to perceive the book as perfect, even though we know it isn't, but that doesn't mean it *isn't*. (Right?) In the next book, we will learn how to lose weight and teach animals to give each other blow jobs . . . Good luck. Godspeed. I love you. Now love yourself.

The End

Acknowledgments

"One of my favorite things is thanking people. It's a kind (and low cost) way to make those who helped you know they're appreciated."
—Eugene Mirman, talking to himself, July 27, 2008

There are a lot of people who made this book possible (not counting Bob Dylan and Lenny Bruce).

Mostly, I'd like to acknowledge the massive all-around-helpfulness, cuddling, and illustration work of Katie Westfall-Tharp. Thank you very much for your many, many hours of listening to my various fake (and spot on) ideas and for bringing my retarded jokes to graphically illustrated life. You're wonderful, and I love you.

I'd like to thank my editor, Allison Lorentzen (I think that's her name), whose feedback and guidance throughout this process was invaluable (I hope that word means very valuable—it does, I just looked it up!). Thank you very much. I could not have done this without you—literally (every book needs an editor who works at a publishing company) and figuratively (your insights and suggestions were invaluable—I know—I should not have used the word again, but it's so *fucking* accurate!).

I'd like to thank Megan Jasper for letting me stay in her wonderful converted garage and write some of my goofy book surrounded by all her taxidermy.

I'd like to thank my friends Matt Savage, Ben Dryer, and Yuli Friedman for reading some early drafts and giving me feedback and encouragement.

I'd like to thank Olivia Wingate for her friendship, guidance, management, and general Britishness.

I'd like to thank Konst, who I sat at Tea Lounge with brainstorming jokes and pop culture references while rewriting the final draft. Also, welcome to America.

I'd like to thank my agent, Rebecca Sherman, for e-mailing me to see if I had a literary agent. I didn't! But now I do. Thanks for helping me craft the proposal and sell the book.

I'd like to thank my kitty-cat, Burton, who wrote one sentence of the book, but sat on my desk as I wrote the rest.

I'd like to thank the Lexington public school system for teaching me English, because this book would have made little sense in a private language of my own creation (which—despite the film *Nell*—is impossible according to Wittgenstein).

I'd like to thank Hampshire College for providing a confusing, but extremely rewarding education. Thank you for admitting me, even though I had terrible grades and probably seemed unstable.

And thanks to my fans who will hopefully grow to a number large enough for me to buy a small house on a cute beach—which will reside on top of a giant house on that beach—and have a high speed train that goes from it to my mansion in New York—where I will eat and fuck whatever I want until the end of time.

Thank you.

Index

Compiled by Author

G